THE GIRL

WHO LOOKED BEYOND

THE STARS

The Sheena Meyer Series
Book One

JOA PRESS
FLORIDA

Books by L. B. Anne

LOLO AND WINKLE SERIES

Book One: Go Viral

Book Two: Zombie Apocalypse Club

Book Three: Frenemies

Book Four: Break London

Book Five (Coming Soon): Middle School Misfit

THE SHEENA MEYER SERIES

Book One: The Girl Who Looked Beyond the Stars

Book Two: The Girl Who Spoke to the Wind

ISBN: 9781700075727

Why does the night sky sparkle? Because each star is a jewel carried by an angel.

-Anonymous

L. B. ANNE

1

I never wanted to be special. Most kids find me, uh, different. I guess that's the best way to put it. It's a compliment, if you ask me. Who wants to be just like everybody else? I don't. That would make me predictable, and that would be bad. Nope, I have to keep people on their toes, wondering what I'm going to do next.

Anyway, it turns out I *am* special. What's special about me, you ask? It's nothing you can tell by looking at me. That's for sure.

A few months ago, I found out I'm a—Well, let me tell you a little about me first.

My name is Sheena. I'm thirteen years old, and five-foot-two for now. I'm hoping to grow about seven more inches. I hang upside down by my feet on my dad's inversion table, willing it to stretch me. It could happen. My dad is six-foot-two. That means it's in my genetic makeup to be tall, I hope.

I have curly dark brown hair. Online they call it a 3A curl pattern. My mom won't let me flat-iron it. But I'm a teenager now, right? Shouldn't I be allowed to try new things?

Not in my house.

My dad is all, "You're not walking around looking like some hoochie."

"Straight hair doesn't make me a hoochie, Dad. I just want to switch things up now and then. That's what girls do," I say.

And then my mom chimes in, "You're not a follower—"

"Mom, I didn't say anything about following anybody!"

"—And your hair is fine," she continues. "I'm not going to let you start damaging it with heat."

Ha! I snuck and flat-ironed it anyway. I learned how on YouTube. My mom was—well, she doesn't like me using this word, but it begins with a P and rhymes with hissed. Let's just say my mom was peeved. She threw water on my hair, ruining it.

Can you believe she sent me to school with a half curled-half straightened head of hair? I had to walk around like that all day. That did wonders for my reputation. Sheesh, it's my hair, but I have no say in how it's styled until I'm fifteen.

I don't know why I just went off on that hair trip. At least it shows you what I deal with around here. My house is not a democracy, and my parents are a united front.

Other than the occasional arguments with my parents, my life is pretty mundane. It revolves around school, where I'm not afraid to speak up and will protest anything I have question with, and after-school activities that I often pout through—at first—because my parents force me to participate in them. I think they try to keep me busy because I'm an only child and tend to drive them crazy. There's no way they could handle two of me.

I sound pretty normal, right? Well keep reading, and whether you believe me or not, this is really happening.

I used to stare out the window at the weeping willow in our backyard for hours when I was little. When the wind blew the branches, it reminded me of a woman's hair blowing from her face. I even drew a face on the bark and called her Lani. No one believed me when I told them I saw something glowing among the fluttering silver-backed leaves of the tree.

My mom says I described it as stars or something. They told me I dreamed it. Now I don't even remember what I saw.

Funny how I just thought of that. It's been nine years. I was four then. The willow's branches no longer resemble hair. They blow in waves as if they dance to music, like the murmuration of starlings.

Now, as I watch my willow, a shiver runs through me. Hands reach around and grab my arms.

She didn't say boo or anything but shook me in an attempt to scare me.

"Nice try, Mom."

She rubbed my arms up and down while looking past me. "The wind is really picking up out there. There's a lot of rain heading this way over the next few days. We need it, though."

"Mom, wouldn't it be cool if fairies lived in our willow?"

"Huh, fairies?"

"Mom, don't laugh. Really, what would you do if you saw one?"

"Sheena, please spare me the crazy right now," she said with a laugh as she leaned forward, flipping her head over and re-wrapping the towel around her wet hair.

"Mom," I sang in that way that pleaded with her to answer the question. "Just humor me. I'm an only child. I have no one else to ask these things."

She pursed her lips, giving me her I'm-not-falling-for-that expression. "Okay. I guess I would run."

I giggled. "No, you wouldn't."

"Yes, I would. They may not look like the cute little things you've seen in fairytales."

"Running would be the wrong thing to do. You would miss a great opportunity."

My mom walked through the family room and toward the kitchen. "Come and help me with dinner. What opportunity?"

I followed her to the center island, where vegetables rested on a chopping board. "An opportunity to ask questions, and maybe make a new friend. What about a vampire?"

"Sheena…"

"Just answer for fun."

"I would run."

I shook my head. "Mom, you're not even thinking. You can't outrun a vampire. That would be another missed opportunity."

"An opportunity to get killed," my mom stated as she put on oven mitts and removed a glass pan of bubbling lasagna from the oven and placed it on the stovetop.

"No, for knowledge."

"How did I raise a child that scolds me about how I address vampires?"

"You can't be afraid of everything," I replied as I sliced the cucumber for our salad.

From the corner of my eye, I saw movement.

"Mom?"

"Yes?"

"What are you doing?"

"What does it look like?"

"Mom, stop dancing."

"Oh, I'm going to dance, and you're going to watch. Do you know why?"

"Why?"

"Because you've put that vampire stuff in my head, and now I'll be thinking about it for the rest of the night. If I have to think about vampires, you have to think about me dancing."

"No, not the Running Man! My eyes, my eyes!" I screamed while squeezing my eyes shut.

"Okay, okay," she said with a hand on top of her head. She'd been trying to hold the towel still as she danced. "Whew, thirty seconds of that tired me out. I could do that dance all day when I was younger."

"Much younger."

She threw a piece of carrot at me that I dodged and picked up from the floor. "Look, why don't you focus on chopping that last bit of cucumber before you cut yourself, then go and get ready for the purity ceremony tonight. Wear the white dress. I'm serious."

"Okaaaay, what time do I take my vow of virginity?" I asked and bowed with my palms together as if I were praying.

"Vow of purity," she corrected. "Seven-thirty, and don't make fun. You need to take this seriously."

"I am, just don't tell the boys at school that I am to remain a virgin until marriage. Do you think I'd have a better chance of a vampire wanting my blood because I'm pure?"

"Oh my gosh, forget the cucumber. Get out of my kitchen," she replied as she turned on the cold water and used the sink spray nozzle to shoot it at me.

I screamed and ran. I always took things that extra mile just to make my mom laugh. Little did I know, it would be a long time before she laughed like that again.

2

"**M**rs. Meyer, you can go in now."
I rose from my seat, but my mom didn't move. She sat staring straight ahead at the closed blinds of the window across from us. Dried streaks of mascara covered her cheeks from crying. Hugging her was the only thing I could think of to console her, so I hugged her again. This time, she hugged me back and stood.

I'd cried too, all the way to the hospital. I kept picturing myself as my dad, driving down the highway at night. But I could also see the car approaching from the other direction and the young driver looking away from the road to tap on his GPS. I could see my dad swerve away to avoid the impact. But the road was wet, and the other car kept spinning...

I was so angry at first at the thought of my dad being taken away from me. The tears started, but I stopped crying because I had to believe my dad was okay. And if I believed, that meant no more tears. So I blew my nose, wiped my eyes, and covered my ears with my headphones, blocking out my mom's sobs.

"This way," said the nurse.

I tried to read the nurse's expression to get some idea of how my dad was, but there was none. She had to be a gambler, because she had the best poker face ever. Her expression was blank and empty like she'd never had an emotion. She didn't look us in the eye or even at face level. Instead, she glanced in our direction and over our heads as she held the door.

I ran back and got my mom's purse she'd left on the chair. She'd been forgetting everything since the accident, thirty-six hours ago.

We followed the nurse through double doors, down a hallway, around two corners, and down an even longer hallway. I hoped my mom would remember the way out, because I felt like we were in a maze.

The nurse approached a door on her left. I let go of my mom's arm and walked in behind them.

My breath caught in my throat and lumped there.

Did I really want to see my dad yet? What if he was all cut up and bloody from the windshield? I closed my eyes, bracing myself, and listened. My mom's reaction would tell me how bad it was.

The room was full of noises, as if it were alive. A machine bleeped every few seconds as if it were a heartbeat. A constant hum came from another machine, and a gurgle from a machine to my right, which was like the breathing of the live room.

My mom spoke to someone. I opened my eyes and watched her shaking hands with a man in a white coat, one of the doctors.

"He's still unconscious, but he's breathing on his own and..."

That's the last thing I heard the doctor say.

That lump moved deeper into my throat. My eyes drifted from the white sheet that covered my dad, to one of his legs lifted, and in a cast, up to his bandaged head, and the tubing in his nose.

I gasped, seeing the cuts and scrapes on his face, and the swelling. He didn't look like himself. I wasn't even certain that was really him.

A tear dropped from my eye and rolled down my cheek. My mom must have noticed, because I felt her hands on my shoulders.

"He's going to be okay," she whispered.

Okay? What I saw was not okay.

My eyes were still on his face, memorizing it, and comparing it to the once handsome features I could no longer see.

A flash of light broke my focus. I looked from my dad's face, up above him, to the ceiling. My knees buckled, and I stumbled to the side and back a couple steps into the chair by the door.

My mom caught me. "Breathe, Sheena, breathe. Maybe I should take her out."

The doctor asked me something, but I couldn't nod or speak. I wanted to, but that lump in my throat grew and cut off my air supply.

I wanted to point and yell, "Look!"

My mom looked back at my dad, but she didn't have the reaction I had. Why not? Why wasn't she ready to run as she always claimed she would if she saw something unusual—a creature?

Over my dad stood a being. I didn't know what else to call it. It was white, but not like the color white—kind of translucent with a glow like a blue current ran through it.

I watched as it waved a huge hand over my dad's head, passing right through it. I couldn't believe my eyes.

My dad blinked.

"Look," I finally yelled, shocked I'd actually spoken that time.

My dad's eyes slowly opened.

"Jonas, I'm here," my mom said as she ran to his bedside and held his hand. "Jonas, can you hear me?"

My dad tried to nod.

Why is she ignoring the thing behind him looking down at them?

The being backed away—like backing through the wall, and as he did so, he began to disappear.

"Wait!"

"Wait for what? What's wrong?" asked my mom, hearing the alarm in my voice. Tears streamed down her face again, but she wasn't sad anymore. These were happy tears.

"I need some air. Out there." I pointed behind me. My voice shook. "Can I go out in the hall for a minute?" I didn't wait for a reply.

I looked both ways in the hall. The thing backed out, which would have taken it to the left if it were going to the next room or down the hall. I turned the corner, as there were no other rooms behind my dad's.

I argued with myself the whole time. *What am I doing? Why am I looking for this thing? It could just disappear. It doesn't need to go down a hall like a human walking.* Still, I searched.

My mom, the doctor, and the nurse saw nothing. That meant I could have imagined it. But I didn't. I needed to see it again to prove to myself it was real.

At the end of the hall, near tan double doors, I saw a zip of light and followed it.

"Wait!" I yelled as I turned the corner.

The light hovered near the ceiling as if waiting. Instead of the appearance of a bright electric current, it morphed into a formless glob of light.

I glanced behind me. Except for me, and this thing, the hall was empty.

My heart raced. I readied myself to bolt in the other direction if it headed for me. Yeah, I know. I'd told my mom she should never run.

My hand flew up, shielding my eyes from the flash of light that blinded me for a moment as the being began to form itself again, only this time it was less transparent and filled with more light. It had to be, like, nine feet tall.

I slowly stepped toward it, having an overwhelming feeling I didn't need to be afraid.

Although the being didn't necessarily have an expression or facial features, so to speak, it angled its head down and looked at me.

"Hi," I said nervously.

I got the feeling it couldn't believe I could see it or that I was talking to it. When I was just a few feet away, and could really see the magnitude of it, I reached down into my pocket and slowly pulled out my phone. As I held it up to snap a photo, it disappeared.

What was I thinking? "No, wait. Look, I put it away. I saw what you did. Come back!" My voice dropped. "I just wanted to...meet you and...say thank you."

I looked around at the ceiling and waited.

Nothing.

I must have stood there for ten minutes. It was just gone.

"That was so stupid. Stupid, stupid, stupid," I yelled while popping myself on the side of the head. "A once in a lifetime manifestation or something, and you try to take a picture? What, so you can post it online, or on some underground alien sighting website? Really? Ugh! How stupid are you?" I yelled while turning in a half-circle, stomping my feet and swinging at the air.

"Hello," came from behind me.

3

I froze in place, hearing the man's voice. Had he heard me talking to myself? Or was it him—the being?

Oh my gosh-oh my gosh-oh my gosh, I thought as I took a deep breath and slowly turned, frightened and excited at the same time. I was actually about to talk to this— whatever it was—an apparition, or something.

He leaned on a cart with some type of equipment and a computer monitor on it. He had caramel skin like mine, short curly hair, and wore grey scrubs.

"I'm Javan. It's nice to meet you."

"Hello," I replied to the nurse while looking around him.

He smiled in a way that made me feel he wanted to burst with laughter, having heard what I'd been saying. If he mentioned it, I was going to drop dead right then and there.

"Looking for something?"

"No, I thought—no, I have to get back to my dad." He pulled the cart out of the way and watched me walk around him and down the hall.

"You're not lost, are you? I can help you, or have another nurse help you?"

"No, I know the way, thank you."

My chin sunk to my chest. I couldn't believe I messed up that opportunity. I looked back once more before turning the corner. Javan watched me and waved. He had a really nice smile. I waved back and bumped into a wheelchair as I turned around.

"Oops, sorry!"

"What did you see?"

"Huh?"

"You were down there a long time. You still have a residual proximity glow. You saw him, didn't you?"

The old man had thin white hair that hung to his shoulders and the strangest twinkle in his eye. "A lot of unexplainable things go on around this place." He leaned forward in his chair and whispered. "I think he was assigned here."

"Who?"

"Mr. Tobias, are you harassing this young lady?"

"No, ma'am. Only you, Nurse Rita."

She laughed. "Good, let's get you back to your room."

"I got out here by myself, didn't I?"

"You're not even on the right floor."

"Oh. Well, this is where all the action happens." He winked at me.

I watched him being wheeled away.

"There aren't many special ones like us," he yelled behind him. "We're the last. May your vision be true, Little Gleamer!"

Little Gleamer? That was weird. I turned the corner to get back to my dad's room. My pace slowed.

Like us? The last? The last what? Hmph, crazy old man.

"Sheena," my mom called from the other end of the hall. "Where did you go? Don't you want to see your dad? I know it's hard to see him like this—"

"No, I just needed to—How *is* Daddy?"

"It's a miracle from heaven."

Those last words started my mind going all over again. *A miracle from heaven. HEAVEN?*

My dad was able to smile a little. I mean, the normal person wouldn't know it was a smile. It looked more like a grimace. I had made a joke, telling him if he didn't want to start teaching me to drive, he could've just told me instead of wrecking his car. His mouth quivered a little and then the right side shifted up just a tad, and then down. That was the grin. He couldn't talk, but he knew who we were and that was a big deal. It wouldn't be long before he would be able to come home.

It was early morning when we left the hospital because we'd stayed all night, but I didn't care that I hadn't had any sleep. When I got to my room, I went straight to my laptop. I looked up heaven and happened upon angel sightings. Was it possible that's what I saw? An angel?

My mind flashed back to Mr.— *What did she call him?* Tobias. He said he was assigned here and something about us being special. He sounded delusional to me, but if he wasn't, did he mean here, as in the hospital, or here, as in the city of Muskegon?

"Sheena," my mom called from the hall. "Are you in bed?"

"Yes!"

I reached over, switched off my table lamp, and pulled my blanket up over me and the laptop. "Okay. Angel sightings. What have we got?" I whispered to myself and typed it in the search engine.

Angels are spiritual beings believed to act as an attendant, agent, or messenger of God. They guide and protect people. They are represented in human form having halos, wearing long robes, with majestic wings.

That's not what I saw, I thought as I clicked on an image, expecting to find more valuable information. But what I found was a bunch of stupid stuff. Angels formed in clouds and images on walls by the way the light shined on it. "So, pretty much you're saying, 'Oh, look at those clouds. Doesn't that look like an angel?' or, 'Hey, look how the floodlight makes it look like there's an angel on the wall.' This is stupid."

I give up, I thought after an hour of unsuccessful research. If I didn't know any better, I would have believed someone was purposely blocking me from finding any information.

My mouth opened in a huge yawn. If I didn't get to sleep soon, I would be like the walking dead later that day when it was time to go back to the hospital.

I shut the laptop and said a prayer for my dad.

When I was little, my mom told me that if you sang to the heavens at night, angels would visit you and protect you. It's funny how I just began remembering things like that.

I knelt in front of my window, looking up at the stars with my head resting over my folded arms, and sang as quietly as I could so my mom wouldn't know I was still up. "I'll search for you. I look beyond the stars and find your glory. Here's my honor," I sang. A song my mom taught me years ago. Well, she didn't actually teach me. She sang the words so often that one day while she was singing it while washing dishes, I overheard her from the family room and when she paused, I continued the song and we finished it in unison. She was shocked.

I waited at the window a few minutes. I guess I thought an angel would materialize in front of me. I mean, why else did I sing? I laughed at myself for thinking like the four-year-old me and climbed into bed.

As I lay on my side, I pulled my covers up, forming my cocoon, and sighed into the pillow. My dad was alive. I felt grateful and at peace.

I closed my eyes, exhausted, and ready for sleep to find me. A few seconds later, my eyes shot open.

Someone's in my room!

I could feel it. I tried to look behind me without turning or moving and opened my mouth to scream for my mom, but nothing came out.

There's an intruder in my room and there's no one to help me! My eyes scanned over every inch of the room in front of me for a weapon. The nightstand was too far away to reach for the lamp. Beyond the nightstand was a closet and shelves of books, stuffed animals, and everything I'd collected since I was about five years old. There was nothing I could reach for to hit someone with. Why wasn't I into baseball or softball? Then I would at least have a bat.

My heart pounded hard in my chest and then in my ears, blocking out every other sound. I couldn't decide if I should wait for a hand to reach out and grab me or turn and face whoever it was.

Get up, Sheena! I yelled in my head. I shot towards my lamp, switched it on with a tap, picked it up, and swung it around. I was going to pulverize whatever was coming for me.

The room was totally empty.

My shoulders raised and lowered with my breaths. I looked down at the lamp pointed at the door and suddenly became aware of what I looked like standing there in my t-shirt, pajama pants covered in pink hearts, and my fluffy pink socks, shaking and ready to fight—or run. I felt so foolish. My mom would say, "That's why you don't look up that kind of stuff before going to bed." She was right.

I put the lamp back and laid down, this time facing the door. Although the room was getting brighter due to daylight, I left the lamp on. But when I awoke, the lamp was switched off.

4

M y life was boring as kids' lives go, and then *WHAM*. Of all the unlikely things that could happen to me, to anyone, this happened. I couldn't stop thinking about it, and I couldn't eat. Well, I could've eaten pizza, but my mom didn't offer me pizza. She offered me overnight oats. *Blech!*

There was investigating to do, and there was nothing I liked more than wearing my investigator's hat. Not a real hat, just a mode I went into when I wanted to figure something out. It's practice for when I become a detective, or a reporter, or an attorney, or an archaeologist—I couldn't make up my mind.

My parents don't care what I become as long as I own the company. My dad says kids today focus on working for someone else. And that becomes a whole four-hour rant about my future. But you know what? I'd rather have my dad shouting to the heavens about his expectations for me than to have him near death in the hospital.

I didn't have to go to school that day or the next, and that was fine with me. We went back to the hospital to see my dad.

In the car, I looked over at my mom. Her hair was pulled up in a bun. She wore no makeup and had bags under her eyes. She seemed deep in thought.

"Mom?"

"Yes," she responded from a faraway place.

"Do you remember what I was like as a four-year-old— I mean the things I did and everything?"

She smiled at the road. "I remember it all." After a few seconds, she added, "Why do you ask?"

"I'm starting to remember things from that time."

My head jerked forward as she slammed on the brakes. The car screeched to a stop.

"Mom!"

"What things?"

"Mom, are you trying to kill me?" I looked around us at the intersection. Cars were lined up behind us and honked like we didn't know the light was green.

"You're blocking traffic. Why would you slam on the brakes like that? Now I have whiplash!"

My mom laughed. "You don't have whiplash." She continued down the road. "Is there something in particular you remember?"

"No, not really. Just bits and pieces of things that I hadn't thought about in years. Like our willow. There's something about our willow," I said almost to myself.

We were now at a red light, and my mom stared at me but didn't say anything.

"What's wrong?"

"Nothing. Just noticing you're not much different than you were at four. You're bigger, but you look exactly the same." She ran her hand over my hair and smiled, but I noted a hint of concern or worry in her expression.

My dad's recovery in one night was amazing. He wasn't sitting up or anything, but he was aware of everything and sucked on ice chips. While my mom read to him, I went to find a candy machine and thought just maybe I might run into Mr. Tobias again.

No, I really just wanted to see if Mr. Tobias would say any other weird stuff. Maybe he could explain what he thought we both saw or what he meant by gleamer.

"Are you lost?" asked a nurse.

"No, I'm looking for Mr. Tobias."

"Who?"

"The old man in the wheelchair? He was here last night. Early this morning, really. He was on the wrong floor?"

She laughed. "Oh yes, he's gone home, but I'm sure he will figure out a way to get back here as soon as he can."

"Why?"

"I don't know. He likes it here for some reason." She walked away.

"Excuse me, nurse?"

She turned back. "Yes?"

"Do you know Nurse Javan?"

She looked up at an angle as if she were trying to remember something. "I don't think I do. Is she on this floor?"

"He's a male nurse. He worked last night."

"No, we didn't have a nurse named Javan working last night. Was he cute?" she asked as she walked into the nurse's station.

I shrugged. "I don't know."

The nurse checked her computer and asked others about Javan. "I'm sorry, I have no idea who that could have been."

"Thank you." I turned to head back to my dad's room. *That's so weird. Maybe I imagined it, the whole thing. A nurse no one has heard of, and a giant figure made of pure energy? Who says that was an angel in the first place? But, Mr. Tobias...*

5

With each day that passed, what happened at the hospital seemed more like a dream. Only it was a dream I couldn't shake.

I went back to school and endured the awkward sympathies from students and teachers about my dad's accident. The word sure did get around fast. I walked the halls in a fog, but I didn't really know why. Something was beginning to stir inside me. And I kept having the feeling I was being watched.

"Sheena, are you okay? What are you looking at?"
I tried to see around the backdrop of an exhibit in the gym. "Yeah, what's going on?"

Chana looked confused. "What do you mean, what's going on? They're setting up for career day. This whole thing was your idea!"

"No, I mean with that girl. Over there behind Jeremy. See, she just jumped behind that poster board. I think she's been watching me all morning. Who is she?"

The girl's hair was in shoulder-length twists with the top section secured to the side. She wore a t-shirt and jeans, with a hoodie tied around her waist.

"I don't know. She's new. She started here while you were gone."

"She looks familiar. She keeps looking over here."

"Maybe you should say something to her."

"I would if every time I looked in her direction, she didn't look away or hide behind something."

"Weirdo."

"Ha! You called *her* a weirdo."

"Why is that funny?"

"Because that's what everyone thinks of *me.*"

"Well, let's see. You're always with me, that may be kind of weird, but we're best friends so whatever, we have the best lunches in the state, but you usually bring your lunch while the rest of us buy ours, you say things like pièce de résistance…"

I had to laugh at that part.

"…you look at boys like they have the plague, your mouth always gets you in trouble, you have the strangest taste in music and I'm not mad at you about it—most kids are into hip hop, but you want to listen to Fleetwood Mac."

"It's all about Stevie Nicks. I'm telling you, don't sleep on—"

"I know. I know. Please don't start. You need to stop listening to your parent's satellite radio stations. And let's see, what else? Oh, and you are socially awkward."

"All of that, huh? You just had to go there."

"Maybe you *are* weird."

"Then you are too," I replied as we laughed.

"I'm the outgoing one."

She was right. Chana was everyone's friend, but mainly mine. I may not have been a geek or nerd, but I was certainly not popular. Well, I was popular in the everyone-knows-who-I-am way (It's not important why everyone knew of me. I'm just saying), but not in the everyone-wants-to-be-my-friend way.

I was mostly ignored unless I wore a new hairstyle, or the popular girls decided I looked cute. The last time that happened, they dragged me over and tried to introduce me to Cecil, one of the popular boys that didn't have a girlfriend. I already knew Cecil from elementary school, but he never talked to me in middle school. I guess they were introducing him to what they considered the new improved me—the upgrade. For one whole day, I was like best friends with them. The next day when I went back to my normal self, they ignored me. Whatever. Those weren't the type of friends I wanted anyway. And Cecil...I guess he didn't find my awkwardness attractive.

"Are you coming outside?" asked Chana.

"No. I'm going to the library before class. Are you joining me?" I didn't really want her to, because I didn't want her to see what I was researching, but I had to ask.

"In the library? No, you can have that. I'll see you later."

Chana turned to walk away, and just like that, someone quickly took my place beside her, giggling as they went outside. Oh, to be so likable.

Our school had a great library, but I wasn't interested in books that day. I wanted to continue my investigation. I walked past aisles of books to the computer stations at the back of the room, having the area all to myself until a few boys came in and started horse-playing behind me. Obviously, they only came to the library to get out of going outside after lunch.

A wad of paper hit my head.

"Creep!" I said and faked like I would run after them.

The boys scattered, but they came back a few minutes later. I was glad when they got kicked out, so I could focus.

I started my search again on angels. Nothing I found specifically had to do with seeing an angel. Then I found an article that taught you how to see angels.

Hmmmm... I didn't know that was something that could be taught. I quickly skimmed through the article, trying to hurry before the bell rang for the next period.

"Angels appear as orbs or bright lights, yadda-yadda, they may not have wings, yadda-yadda, they're on a high vibrational frequency. Call in the white light," I whispered, reading aloud. *Nope, not doing that. I don't even know what that means, but that doesn't sound right.*

"Hey!"

WHAM! I jumped, hitting my hand on the side of the desk. "Ouch!"

"Are you okay? I didn't mean to scare you."

"Aww man, I broke my nail."

"I'm Ariel. I'm new here."

I frowned at my hand while examining the nail. "Yes, I heard. I mean, I'm Sheena."

"Sheena? Nice name."

"Thanks. It means God is gracious."

"That's cool that you know the meaning. Mine means lion of God. It is usually used as a boy's name in Hebrew, but in the United States it's the norm for girls—or mermaids."

She laughed at her joke.

I smiled but really wanted to shoo her away like an insect. "I was kind of in the middle of something...I'm not trying to be rude. When I'm working on something, I have to give it my full attention. You understand what I'm saying, right? You'll get used to me."

"No worries. What are you looking up?"

"Oh, nothing." I quickly shut off the computer monitor and powered down the system. I needed to get to class anyway.

"Something about angels?"

"You saw that?"

She nodded with a bright, happy smile.

"Yes, just curious, that's all."

She placed her hand over mine. "No worries. I'd better get going, though. I'm always late to class." She lifted her hand. "See you later, Sheena."

I watched her walk away. *And they say I'm weird. She just put her hand over mine like she was my mom, or Nana or something.* I looked at my hand. "My nail!"

Ariel turned back. "What about it?"

"It's fixed."

She moved in closer to me, smelling of flowers. "Are you sure it was broken? Looking at it, it looks like only your polish was broken, I mean chipped." She shrugged. "See ya."

I meant to respond, but I couldn't stop examining my nail. *I know I'm not going crazy. My nail was broken.* I was so upset about it because I had just started allowing my nails to grow and polishing them with Chana.

"Mom!"

"I'm back here!"

I closed the front door and ran to the back of the house. She sat in the family room, folding clothes while watching television. "What are you so excited about? Was today a good day? You didn't say anything you would regret, as you usually complain you do sometimes, did you? Like how you questioned your science teacher on the existence of atoms that time until he wanted to pull his hair out? You remember that talk we had about you not voicing every single thing that erupts from your brain?"

"No, mom, that didn't happen. Not today, at least. Look! My fingernail was broken and then it went back together all by itself."

She looked up at me. "Are you sure it was broken?"

"Yes."

"Let me see."

I was already scooting in next to her so she could get a closer look.

"Could you at least have taken off your backpack?"

"Oh, yeah, I was in a hurry to tell you."

"Okay, I see the polish scraped right there. Is that where it was broken?"

"Yes." I replied with eyes wide. My arms flew up. "Can you believe it? I've witnessed a miracle!"

She laughed. "I wouldn't exactly call that a miracle. Now, your dad's recovery—that's a miracle."

I stared at her for a moment as she put my stack of folded clothes in a basket and handed it to me. *A miracle, she said. Hmmm...*

"Come to think of it, is that my polish you're wearing?"

I grabbed the basket and hurried down the hall to the stairs. "Sorry Mom, I didn't hear a thing you said, I'm putting my clothes away. And thank you for folding them for me."

6

*T*he new girl, Ariel, stood outside the school near the bicycle racks waving when I arrived the next day. I looked behind me toward the crossing guard. *Is she waving at me?*

"Sheena!" she exclaimed.

Why is she so happy to see me?

"Sorry, I'm always happy to see a familiar face. Why are you looking at me like that?"

"You just responded to what I was thinking."

"I did? That's impossible. How would I know what you were thinking?"

"I don't know. I guess it was a coincidence. Why are you standing around out here?"

"I was waiting for you," she replied with a huge grin.

Her hair was pulled back in a wavy ponytail, revealing a birthmark at her temple that looked like a star. There was something kind of awkward about her. At the same time, she seemed so free, like she didn't have a care or worry in the world. Didn't she know about the plastic straw epidemic or about the increase in homelessness in the city? Or what about the missing kids from the tri-county area? I mean, I was worried about those things. And what about Brexit? I wasn't really sure what Brexit was, but I needed to know how worried I needed to be about it.

I tripped forward after being nudged in the back. The boy jumped away from me in a boxing stance, waiting to see what I'd do—swing at him and/or chase him.

"Hey, leave her alone," yelled Ariel.

I laughed. "It's okay. He's actually my friend. We still hit each other and run like little kids." I took a step toward him, and he ran. "Keep running, butt face!"

"Language, Sheena," said Mr. Haleigha while walking past me.

"Sorry."

Ariel chuckled. "Shall we go in?"

"Shall?" *That was an odd word to use.* "Okay."

We walked into the building and to the same homeroom. "This is you also?"

"Yeah, I switched," Ariel replied.

"I didn't know they do that."

Most of the students ignored us as we entered the classroom, but the teacher smiled up at us from her desk.

"We have a new student. What's your name?"

"Ariel. Ariel Knight."

"Ariel, I'm Mrs. Yancey. I don't see you listed as a new student. Are you sure you're in the correct class?"

"Um-hm, that's what they told me." She handed the teacher a crumpled paper from her pocket. "It's right there on my schedule."

"That it is. Go ahead and have a seat."

"Anywhere?"

"Yes. There's no assigned seating."

Ariel sat two seats over from me in the same row. She seemed happy to be there and watched me often.

It couldn't be easy being new. I've lived in the same house forever, so I've never been the new kid, but I knew these rascals (that's what my mom called my classmates) wouldn't make it easy. I decided I would eat lunch with her if we had the same lunch period and help her get acclimated since it seemed like no one else would. Maybe the office sent a student around with her on her first day, or one of the days I was out. But if they did, why would she be looking for me first thing in the morning? She had to have met other people.

"Ariel, over here!" I stood and waved my hand over my head as I yelled over the constant chatter of the other students in the cafeteria.

"Oh, you know her now?" asked Chana.

Ariel's eyes brightened and her arm shot up in seeing me. "Hey, Sheena. Chana."

"Have we been introduced?"

"Stop it," I whispered. That wasn't like her.

"I remembered your name from social studiesclass."

I positioned myself in front of Ariel, where I could block her off from Chana's eye-roll.

"We have the same lunch period," said Ariel.

"Yeah, have you been introduced to the groups in here?"

"Groups?" She shook her head.

"Within the walls of this cafeteria is a whole society exhibiting dominance patterns in groups."

"She learned that in social studies," Chana said over my shoulder.

"Sure did, and I'm glad I can use what I learned for once in a real-life scenario."

I grabbed Ariel's shoulders and turned her around, facing the room. "Okay, this is a quick who's who in this middle school universe. Those girls are the FPS (fips), the future pop stars—that's what *they* think anyway. They dance, they sing, they're popular, and God forbid they have a hair out of place at any time. As you can see, they try to dress like the stars they're going to be without breaking the school dress code. Some don't care and will arrive in cropped tops and just deal with the consequences. I don't know what they're going to do next year when the school switches to uniforms. As far as they're concerned, they're royalty and we are mere peasants. The one in front, in the blue glittery jersey, I used to be good friends with—"

"Yeah, until she came back from summer break with curves," said Chana. "Then she didn't know Sheena anymore."

"Yeah, I'm still waiting on my curves. Anyway, over there you have the typical geeks, and those guys along the wall are the unmentionables."

"Unmentionables?"

"Yeah, they are mostly ignored, like they don't matter. But truthfully, they're cool. They're just introverts, I guess. Back there, by the door, are the jokers—you know, like in Batman?"

Ariel looked at me like she had no idea what I was talking about.

"They're playful and joke around a lot, which always gets them in trouble. They're harmless, but a little annoying at times. They fart a lot too. They'll make you sorry you ever inhaled."

"Flammable like methane," Chana added.

"Oh, and they beg for your food after they've eaten their own. I guess you need extra calories when you keep up so much mischief.

"Then you have your sporties—basketball, football, soccer—that's all they care about. At that next table, you see the bookworms sitting together. But look at them. They don't talk. They just sit and read. I don't get it. Why bother sitting together? I'm not hating. I'm just saying."

"She's hating," Chana chimed in.

"Those guys over there by the FPS—they're trouble and just mean for no reason at all. I used to be one of them."

"You?" Ariel's eyes were wide with shock.

"I hate to admit it. I went through a rebellious stage, and Chana here had to help me see the error of my ways."

"Yeah, I slapped her and yelled, 'Snap out of it!'" Chana said with a straight face while placing her straw in her drink.

"Anyway, just ignore them and keep it moving."

"Keep it moving," Ariel repeated. "What about you guys?" She looked back and forth from me to Chana. "What group are you in now?"

"The groups she just mentioned form a ring," said Chana, as she drew a circle in the air with her finger. "We fall directly in the center of that ring."

"Meaning you're a little bit of everybody?"

I thought for a moment. "Yeah, I guess we are."

"In all honesty, they probably all want to be us," said Chana.

"We are the crème de la crème," I responded in my best French accent.

"The world is full of lots of interesting people," said Ariel.

"Yeah, that's one way to put it," I replied.

Ariel giggled, "That kid in that group you called 'trouble' just called you a loser."

"That's Cameron. Ignore him. He's just trying to get something started. Keyword, ignore. Ignore, ignore, ignore. Just let things roll off you and you'll be okay."

I sat, and Ariel sat next to me. There was still something familiar about her. It was her eyes. I'd seen them before somewhere.

"That's interesting. Kind of bohemian," I said, noticing her bracelet.

Chana leaned over my sack lunch so she could see also. Ariel covered the bracelet with her hand. "It's nothing. My mom made it."

It was a strange-looking old metal star with several tan ropes that tied it around her wrist.

"Aren't you going to eat anything?"

"No…" she said as she looked around, studying the trays on the table. She sounded unsure.

"We have a good selection for vegetarians, or carnivores like me," said Chana.

Ariel looked down at her lap.

"Here, you can share with me."

"No, that's okay."

"I always bring extra for this reason."

"You bring an extra lunch to give away?"

"Yeah, you never know who may not have lunch and may be afraid or ashamed to ask."

"Even for the jokers?"

"No, they eat. They just want more. But if they hadn't eaten, they could have it. It's for anyone. I may not like a lot of the kids in here, but I don't want them to go hungry."

"That's cool."

"If she gets elected class president, she plans to work on everyone getting free lunches," said Chana.

"Prisoners do, why shouldn't students?"

"That's awesome."

"It's really not a big deal." I pulled two sandwiches out of my bag and held one in each hand. "This one is turkey and cheese, and this one is almond butter and strawberry preserves. Which do you want?"

"I don't know."

"We'll go halfsies then."

She grinned. "Okay."

"Where are you from?" asked Chana as she opened her applesauce and licked the back of the lid.

"Far away. You wouldn't know it."

"Okayyyyy…I suppose middle schools are pretty much the same everywhere, but do you like it here?"

"Yes, and my new friends," she said smiling at me.

She watched me and took a bite of her half sandwich after I did. I almost thought she didn't know how, like she was new to eating.

"This is good."

"I made it myself."

"I know."

"You do?"

"I mean I figured you did. You're old enough. Yum, what is that?" she asked, licking the yellow goo from her lip.

"You've never had mustard?" Chana asked with a laugh.

"Umm... not this kind," Ariel replied, looking slightly embarrassed.

I opened my bag of chips and offered her some. She stared at it. I reached in and took one, and she did too.

"You are very kind."

Three boys rushed over to the table. "Are you coming out?"

"Do you want to go out, Ariel?"

She nodded.

Chana turned in her seat and leaned her back against the table. "I don't understand why we have to go out after lunch like we're kids needing recess."

"I think it's to get us to exercise and move around more. Think about it. We exit through the lunchroom doors and then have to go all the way around the school to the other side of the building to get back in."

"Yes, exercise," Ariel said with her mouth bulging.

As soon as we stepped outside, I realized it may have been a bad idea to take Ariel with me. I hadn't explained the game.

It was warm out. I wrapped and tied the arms of my hoodie around my waist like Ariel's. The boys were waiting just far enough away from the door to give us a chance to run.

"Ariel, do you run fast?"

"Yep."

"I'm no track star but I'm pretty quick. Follow me, and stay close!"

We bolted around trees along the side of the building and jumped onto the bench of a weather-beaten picnic table and sat on the tabletop.

"Dang, watch out," a girl, one of the FPS, exclaimed from the other side of the table.

I think I sat on a few of her waist-long braids that draped over the table.

"Sorry. Excuse us, Bradly," I replied, ignoring her scowl as the boys approached.

"You guys are such toddlers," she replied with a sneer.

"Whatever. That's why she has a boy's name," I whispered to Ariel.

She giggled and turned, watching the other FPS practicing a routine from their dance squad.

"Base," I yelled as the boys made it to the table.

They stopped. "You can't call base every time you run!"

"You know good and well this is always base."

"What's base?" Ariel asked.

I waved my hand in front of us. "Out there is danger and chaos." I tapped the picnic table with the palm of my hand. "But nothing can touch us here. We're safe."

Ariel looked at me in a strange way.

I checked my smartwatch to see how much time we had left before the next period. "The bell is going to ring soon.

We can't stay here forever. We have to make it to the doors to be safe again."

I looked for Chana. She was with the other two girls the boys were chasing. I waved to get her attention, tapped my fists together twice over my head and spread them apart.

Chana held her thumb up and ran. The boys chased after her.

"Come on, we're clear. Let's go."

"She did that for us?" asked Ariel.

"Yep," so we can make it to the building. "Run, Ariel!"

We ran through the crowd that formed in front of the doors and into the building just as the doors opened. I watched for Chana as we stood in the hall against the far wall, catching our breath.

"That was so much fun."

"Yeah, but now I'm all sweaty. Not you though, you still smell like flowers. What is that, your body spray or deodorant?"

"That's the bell. I'll see you later, Sheena."

"Yep, just walk away while I'm talking..."

This is just great! I'm awkward, weird, and now musty. My reputation is just growing leaps and bounds.

"We almost caught you," one of the boys said in passing as he pushed the side of my head.

"Don't make me rub my armpit on you."

Chana ran up behind him and pulled the back of his shirt up over his head. We pushed him back toward the lockers and ran, laughing.

Chana always had my back. You couldn't mess with one of us without having to deal with the other. We bumped fists, crossed arms in the air and brought them down— something we'd been doing for about five years.

"Later, bestie," Chana yelled behind her. "And don't forget to ask your parents about coming over."

7

I was prepared to do some serious whining and begging
to get my mom to let me go to Chana's sleepover. But
I didn't have to. Maybe my mom thought I needed to get
out of the house, or maybe I was getting on her nerves due
to our last conversation. I mean she *did* allow *me* to pick
the movie. I just wanted her to explain why Maleficent was
so huge compared to the other fairies. I didn't get it.

"What's wrong with you?" asked Chana. "You've been
weird lately."

*Weird? Maybe because I saw a creature of some sort, and
this old man told me he saw it too and we're the last of
something. Maybe I should ask my mom if I'm adopted.
Maybe I'm from some alien race.* Those were the kind of
thoughts that went through my head ever since I saw
whatever it was.

"You mean weirder than usual?"

"No, brainiac, the way you've been hanging with that
Ariel girl, and you've been secretive."

"Ariel is sweet. You should get to know her."

"Whatever, just remember I'm the one that has known you since kindergarten. Remember? I stood ground with you when you announced to the whole class that there was no such thing as Santa Claus. Man, you really had everyone upset, including the teacher. Wait, what did you say?"

I mimicked my five-year-old self. "It's imagination." We both laughed as Chana swung a feather boa at me.

Chana was also the one that stopped everyone from calling me a baby in first grade because of the way I talked, and she's always been around ever since in case I need defending, although she never socked someone in the eye again.

"Seriously though, just talk to Ariel and stop being mean."

"I'm not being mean. I talk with you guys at lunch. I'm just saying I've always been here for you and I'll still be here after she moves."

"She's moving?"

"No, I was just hoping."

"Really? This whole jealousy thing is not a good look for you."

"I'm not jealous, and I'm done talking about her. Instead, let's talk about what's really going on—your big secret. It's Theodore, isn't it? You like him, don't you?"

"Teddy? Are you serious? You need to stop overdosing on black licorice."

One long piece hung out of her mouth, and she had five more in her hand.

"We're friends. That's it. Period. Case closed. Don't go there again."

"Okay, got it, dang. But there's something…"

"Isn't he with Georgina?"

"I don't think so."

"Well, they exchanged numbers. He told me."

"Sheesh, he talks too much. Why did he tell you that?"

"Because that's what friends do." My voice trailed off. That's what friends do, I'd said. Now I felt worse. Friends don't keep secrets.

"What's wrong? Was that the secret?" asked Chana.

I went back and forth in my head. *Tell her-don't tell her-tell her-she's your best friend-you're nuts, don't tell her-she'll believe you-tell her...*

We sat facing each other with our legs folded under us. "Okay, this conversation stays right here. I mean you can't tell anyone at all."

"When have I ever? This must be good. Spill…"

I took a deep breath, started to tell her what happened at the hospital, opened my mouth, and what came out was, "Do you believe in…"

Chana leaned in toward me, her hand stopped in midair, her mouth open from where she was about to stuff popcorn in with the black licorice. "What? Do I believe in what? Stop stalling."

"Aliens?"

"Aliens? Well..." she said after throwing popcorn in her mouth. "...I believe there is probably life on other planets. I mean, why should we be the only creatures on a planet?"

"Do you believe in vampires?"

"Sometimes I wonder, you know, because of all the movies." She laid back against a pillow and looked up at the ceiling at a distant place only she could see. "Or maybe I wish one would fall in love with me like in the movies."

"You're goofy. That's like you looking at your licorice and saying, 'I love you, marry me.' In real life, they wouldn't fall in love with their food."

"Wow, you really think about that kind of stuff? Was that it?"

"No." I was embarrassed to actually say it. "What about...Werewolves, shapeshifters, mermaids, Atlantis, elves, fairies?"

"No, no, no, maybe, no, and I wish. Your brain has sure been overactive. I think all this monster talk is a cry for help. I'm calling your mom." She reached for her cellphone and I snatched it away from her. "You need an intervention," Chana continued. "You've got serious issues. I'm just saying."

She climbed off her giant floor pillow, took a step forward and stopped as if she'd hit a brick wall. and stood facing the door. Her body stiffened, as if she'd been turned into stone.

"Chana, what's wrong?" I asked, but she didn't respond. I walked around her facing her. Her eyes were focused in front of her and downward like I wasn't there.

I grabbed her arms. "Chana!"

She wasn't breathing. Black goo ran from her mouth and down onto her chin.

I almost shrieked. My best friend had just turned into a zombie! I shook her, thinking I could snap her out of it.

The dribble flowing from her mouth caused her to lose her deathly stare. She looked at me with an empty I-don't-know-who-you-are kind of expression.

Slowly, she began to grin.

I punched her arm. "You make me sick!"

Chana flinched and laughed while wiping the liquified licorice from her face. "You started it with all your monster talk. I'm still telling your mom."

"Believe me, she already knows," I replied, following her downstairs to the kitchen.

Chana opened the refrigerator, handed me a couple cans of pop, and pulled out a tray of candied yam cupcakes.

"We're OD'ing on sugar tonight? Is that the plan?"

"That's always the plan," she laughed. "Besides, my mom bought all this food and will just be so upset if we eat it all in one night. I can't take that away from her. But listen, you're always in the library, did you read something that made you think that stuff exists?" She sounded excited. Maybe it was the sugar rush.

"No, I just wondered what other people think about that stuff."

We grabbed the cold leftover pizza, ice cream, pretzels, and mini candy bars and tiptoed back to Chana's room in our footed pajamas, looking like two giant toddlers that just robbed a convenience store. Chana held a finger to her lips for us to be quiet as we passed her parents' room.

Once we were on her bedroom floor under our makeshift tent again, I laid back, looking up through the sheer fabric at the twinkle lights, and asked, "What about angels?"

"What about them?"

"Do you believe in angels?"

"Heck no," Chana replied while biting into a slice of cold pepperoni pizza.

"No?" I leaned up on my elbow. "How could you not believe in angels? I would believe in angels before all that other stuff."

"If there were angels walking around, don't you think they would do something to help people? Like with that boy that was in the news that disappeared from Norton Shores a few weeks ago, or like your dad's accident. And you'd think someone would see an angel at some point, and—Sheena? What's wrong? Why are you looking at me like that?"

"I did. I mean I, uh...I think I saw one."

8

"There's no way you saw an angel!" Chana yelled, almost choking on her pizza crust.

"Shh… I did."

"Where?"

"At the hospital."

"When your dad was there?"

I nodded. "Yes, two weeks, one hour, and twenty minutes ago."

"Punk!" She exclaimed as she punched me.

"Ow!"

"It's been over two weeks? Why didn't you tell me?"

"I haven't told anyone. I didn't want anyone to think I was crazy."

"I'm not just anyone. What did you see? I mean, what did it do?"

"I think it helped heal my dad. He's already home from the hospital. That shouldn't even be possible this soon."

"You better not be playing with me right now."

"No, I'm serious."

"Swear."

"You know I don't swear."

"Okay, whatever, just calm down and tell me everything."

"Calm down? You're the one all worked up." I laughed.

"Well, why aren't you?"

"It was two weeks ago. Things tend to be less dramatic as time passes."

I told Chana about the sighting and about the old man. She listened intently, as if I was a hobbit telling the story of my latest adventure.

And after the whole crazy story, she sat up straight, picked up the pint of ice cream we'd brought to the room, and said, "Sounds like an alien encounter to me," as if even an alien encounter happened every day.

"I don't think so. Yes, a celestial being, but...Something from beyond the stars."

"Celestial...Good word. But an angel? Really?"

"I've been researching angels ever since."

Chana looked around the room like she was trying to figure something out. "He said you glowed, the old man? Maybe he was seeing things. If it's true, that would've been cool to see."

"I think he was the only one that could see a glow. He's the only one that mentioned it. Oh, and he said we're, meaning him and me, the last."

"The last what?"

"I don't know. That's why I looked for him at the hospital the next day. I thought maybe I could find out if he was, you know, delusional, or if he could tell me more."

"What if he's not delusional? Are you?"

"Of course not."

"Are you on drugs?"

"No! Why would I be on drugs?"

"Hallucinating?"

"No."

"Schizoid?"

"No."

"That means you saw what you saw. You're certain, right?"

"Yes. I mean I saw *something*."

"Then we need to find Mr. Tobias...From what he said, that wasn't the first occurrence. We need to find out what he knows."

"We? What do you mean, *we*?"

"Since when do I let you go through things alone? This is a miracle."

"You really believe me?"

"Why wouldn't I? You're a little loco, chica," she said with a Spanish accent. "But you've never lied to me—to your parents maybe, but not to me. Plus, you're not the only one that saw it."

She turned toward the flat round object on her desk. "Alexa, where are the angels?"

"The Angels are based in Anaheim, California."

We both fell back laughing. "Wait, it *is* talking about the baseball team, right?"

As usual, Chana always ran her mouth about how she's going to stay up all night, crawl onto the roof from the attic window, and watch the sun come up. Not that night. Not any night. She never makes it. Even after what I'd told her, she fell asleep in the middle of the movie we were watching.

The film was about an angel that decided to become human because he fell in love with a girl. Then she died. Moral of the story, life sucks sometimes.

I turned off the television and laid back on my pillows, watching drops of rain hit the windows. Hearing the rain made me think of my willow tree at home, but I don't know why.

I pictured the branches blowing in the wind, and then I started to remember something, but lighting struck outside Chana's window.

I sprung up.

There was no thunder, but the lighting was getting closer. I could tell because the flash outside the window was growing as if it were heading for the house.

"Chana!" I kicked at her leg. I needed her to see this too, then I'd know I wasn't going crazy.

"Murphin puff," she mumbled in her sleep. Who knows what that meant.

"Chana!"

"Snop gerume."

She made no sense at all. Some help she was.

Another flash.

My head jerked toward the window. I couldn't turn away. I felt like it held me captive. The light started below the window and rose higher, getting brighter as it approached.

No, I don't want this. I don't want this! I yelled in my head as I squeezed my eyes shut. *Missed opportunity,* I heard in my head. That's what I had told my mom. Who cares? I didn't want to see whatever it was.

The room was very still. My heart beat like I'd just run a marathon. I opened my eyes. The only light shone from the twinkle lights overhead.

Footsteps came from down the hall and stopped outside the door. I pulled a blanket up to my eyes, waiting for whatever was coming.

The door creaked open. My heart pounded wildly.

"Are you okay?"

It was Chana's dad.

"Yes, sir."

"Did I wake you?"

I shook my head.

"I just got home. Chana threatened to stay up all night. I'm just checking to see if she made good on that. I see she didn't make it."

"She never does."

"I know. Goodnight."

The door closed.

I sunk back into my pillow, feeling so foolish. The light I saw must of come from her dad driving his patrol car up the long drive to the garage behind the house.

Whew, I was glad Chana hadn't wakened for that. She wouldn't be able to hold a straight face when she looked at me for the rest of the month.

Sleep, where are you, I sang in my head. Why couldn't we have a switch on the side of our heads to shut down our brains when we needed to? I envied Chana being able to fall asleep so easily.

I have a habit of shaking my legs when I'm sitting or lying down. My teachers don't like it. My mom makes me stop at the dinner table by placing a hand over my knee, which makes me realize I'm doing it. Now I lay shaking my leg but didn't realize it until I suddenly stopped. I had a feeling someone was near me, near my feet. My eyes were closed, but I hadn't heard anyone enter the room. Had Chana's dad come in to check on her again?

The hair on my arms stood on end.

I could hear Chana's deep, heavy breathing on my left. I slowly opened my eyes.

Six figures stood in an arc around me and Chana. They were all the same height, but I couldn't make out what they were—just dark figures. They didn't move.

I lifted my head as I looked around and caught a reflection of myself in the mirrored legs of Chana's vanity table. Circles of fire swirled on my forehead. I gasped and brought my hand up to my head, touching one of the circles. It transformed into writing—more like symbols. I couldn't understand its meaning, but it quickly transformed into an image. Two women embraced each other, frightened. Then it disappeared.

I touched another circle, and it, too, went from symbols to an image, and then the third. I didn't get to touch all the circles before they disappeared.

One of the figures moved toward me and grabbed me.

I screamed.

"Sheena! Sheena!" Chana yelled while holding me in the same place the dark figure had grabbed me.

"Huh?"

"You were making crazy sounds in your sleep."

I looked around the room. The light was on, and there was no one there but me and Chana. "Crazier than yours?" I replied with a scratchy voice.

"Whatever. You always say I snore. I don't. Did you have a bad dream?"

"I don't know. I don't remember," I lied. I didn't want to lie to her. I just wanted to process what I dreamed before I discussed it.

I didn't want to go back to sleep. I stared at the ceiling, remembering every single thing about the dream. But sleep eventually overtook me. I awoke with my stomach feeling like someone threw darts from the inside toward my navel.

DING!

"What's that sound?" I groaned. We were still on Chana's floor.

"Your tablet."

I licked my lip. "Wah! What is that? It burns. What's on my lip?"

"Wasabi."

"Sheesh, grow up." It was like the spice opened every pore in my face and bore a hole through my nostrils.

"Breakfast!" Chana's mom called over the intercom.

"No, no breakfast. I can't eat. My stomach feels like a junk food trash heap." I opened one eye. "What are you doing?"

"Oh, just watching you sleep with your mouth open."

"No, I wasn't."

"Did you know we swallow like a thousand spiders in our lifetime? Do you ever wake up feeling like there's a hair in your throat? That was probably a spider."

I threw a pillow at her head. "It's too early for this."

"It's not too early for a toothbrush."

"Haha, you need one just as much as I do. Your breath smells like hot toe jam."

Chana laughed. "That's gross. How do you know what that smells like?"

I sat up and removed my satin cap from my head, releasing my curls as I shook my hand through them. How they fell was how they would stay. I didn't feel like doing anything further to my hair.

"What are you typing? Homework?"

"Nope, not homework. I think I found your Mr. Tobias."

"No, you didn't," I exclaimed as I maneuvered next to her and squinted at the laptop screen.

"Yes, I did. I think. I tried those apps where you enter a person's name and it gives you info on them, but they would only tell me a Tobias family lives in the city. I would have to register for an account and pay to find out more. Then, being the genius that I am, this morning, look what I did…"

She held her phone up.

"I texted everyone I know asking if a Mr. Tobias lives on their street."

"I don't understand. Why would you do that?"

"Most people are all neighborly, so they know just about everyone on the block. I mean, we have block garage sales and parties. Don't you know the names of most of the families on your block?"

"Well, yeah, I guess. And, you *do* know everybody."

"That's right, and guess whose street he lives on?"

"Whose?"

"Your boyfriend, Theodore's. We can ride our bikes over there."

"I can't believe you found him!"

I rolled over to my backpack, hearing my tablet ding again. "Teddy is not my boyfriend," I said with an eye-roll, and opened my tablet. I figured since my phone was dead and my texts were coming to my tablet, it was probably just my mom.

"Chana..." I called, my voice high pitched and soft. I pushed the tablet away.

"What's wrong? Give me that." Chana snatched the tablet from my lap. "What the heck is going—" She fell silent as she read. "Nooooooo..."

"You see it too, right?"

"Is this a joke?"

"It can't be. Remember, no one knows about this, but you...The angel texted me."

9

"*I* just got chills. There's no way this is happening," said Chana.

She read the message aloud. "'Hello, Gleamer. Do not be afraid. You are chosen. If you lose your life, you will find it. Your guide is coming.'"

"Chana, it's going to take me! I'm going to be abducted!"

"Mom!" Chana yelled.

"Don't call your mom!"

Chana jumped up and ran in place. "We have to do something!"

I jumped onto her bed. My eyes frantically searched her room as if the answer was right there, but I just needed to find it. "Okay, okay. Let's go with what you were doing. Mr. Tobias. Let's go with that."

"How do you know something is not going to pop out of thin air and take you right now?"

"It could've done that already."

Chana grinned. "I know what this is. It's Theodore playing a practical joke on you. He's such a numbskull, as my dad would say. This has his name written all over it."

"It's not Theodore. I told you, you're the only person I've told about this."

"Oh, right." Chana read the message again. "If you lose your life, you will find it? That could mean if I kill you, then you'll find life—in a grave! Mom!"

I covered her mouth with my hand. "Stop calling your mom. Calm down." I took a few deep breaths. "I really don't think I'm in danger."

Chana looked at me unbelievingly. "You question everything, but this is fine with you?"

"Why now? Two weeks *after* the sighting? I don't—" Images from last night's nightmare flashed through my mind. It was all connected somehow. "Let's just check out Mr. Tobias," I continued, trying to sound as sure and calm as I could.

Although Chana's mom's French toast smelled like pure vanilla sunshine, I didn't bother eating breakfast. I dressed quickly, leaving Chana at the table pouring syrup over my portion as well as hers, and went home to get my bike.

"You just spent all night with her. Haven't you seen enough of Chana?" my mom asked.

"Never," I said as I lifted my leg over the seat of my bike. I looked up seeing Dingy, the little boy next door, looking out the window at me. He waved and I nodded my head up toward him.

"I'm going to talk to your dad again about you needing a sibling."

"It's too late for that," I yelled behind me.

As I rode up the street, my pocket vibrated. I looked at my phone.

ON THE WAY

Why does she always text in all caps?

At the end of the block, I turned left and saw Chana pedaling up the hill. I smiled, relieved that I finally had someone to share this experience with. Though I didn't know why she rode all the way to me. We would have to double back past her house to get to Monroe Street, where Theodore lived.

Now here's the thing about our town, it's hard for kids to do anything without getting caught.

We live in Muskegon, Michigan. If you hold your right hand up, with your palm facing you, that would be the shape of Michigan, a mitten. Muskegon is located halfway up the left edge of the mitten, on Lake Michigan. It's a small town where everybody knows just about everybody or is related to just about everybody. That means if you're seen doing anything wrong, chances are it will get back to some member of your family. Or someone that knows your family will chastise you just like they're your parents. So, you had to be careful—*WE* needed to be careful about whatever we were doing. Like the time Mrs. Jessie ran out of her house and chased us with a switch because she saw us climb from Chana's window into a tree. Chana didn't want to do it. It was my idea, but she went along with me. And Mrs. Jessie was fast. I could feel the whip of the switch slashing through the air behind me as I ran. We got in so much trouble that day.

"Sheena, my love. No. I mean I love you like a sister, but you're not going anywhere with me looking like that."

My hand sprung up to my hair. "Oh my gosh, I forgot to comb my hair."

"Where is your mind at? I knew you weren't really as calm and collected as you were putting on. Has this really got you messed up like that? Sheesh, come here."

I turned my back to her so she could try to do something with my hair.

"I couldn't possibly let Theodore see you looking like this."

"Not funny. Anyway, Teddy has seen me covered in mud from head to toe. This is nothing." I tried to pull away, but Chana's fingers gripped my hair pretty tight, putting two twists in the front and letting the back hang loose.

"Let me look at you," she said, spinning me around.

"Am I presentable now, mom?"

"Yeah, that's better." She licked her thumb and reached for my hairline.

I dodged her hand. "Don't you dare attempt to lay down my edges with your saliva."

"I'm not." Chana laughed pulling back her hand.

We rode our bikes a few blocks down to Theodore's street. "Okay, which house is his?"

"How am I supposed to know? Oh, look," said Chana.

Theodore stood in his driveway. I still had trouble getting used to seeing him without his dreads. I mean, he looked fine without them—very clean-cut, but he'd had them for about four years, and they were so long. It was an adjustment.

"Hey, Teddy."

"Double trouble! What's up?" Teddy replied without looking up from his phone.

"Hey, Theodore. What game are you playing? Fortnite?" asked Chana.

"What else? Battle Royale. You want in on my squad?"

Chana looked around and pointed at herself. "Is he seriously talking to me?"

"You asked."

"No, I don't want to be on your friggen squad."

"Children, play nice," I said, walking my bike between them. Chana and Teddy were friends, but they could only be nice to each other for about two seconds before they found something to disagree about. "Have you forgotten why we're here?"

Chana angled her head around me at Teddy. "You said Mr. Tobias lives on your street, right?"

"Yeah, at the end of the block by the school."

"The brick house?"

"No, the white house next to that one. Wait," he said, backing up his driveway toward his bike. "I'll go with you."

"The Mr. Tobias you know—is he old?"

"Yep, like eighty years old, I think."

"Is he Caucasian?"

"Yep."

"Friendly?"

"I think so. We don't see him much anymore. I think my dad said he's in the hospital a lot."

"Yeah, that's got to be him," I replied.

"What's with all the questions? What do you want with him?" Teddy asked as he rode his bike without using the handlebars until we got to an intersection.

"I-ummm…"

"You are so nosey," Chana accused.

"You came to me for this information, remember?"

"Exactly, information. I just need to ask him a question."

"Something you couldn't ask your parents?"

"They don't know him."

Teddy rolled his eyes. "You know what I'm trying to say. How is your dad, though?"

"Recovering fast. He's home now."

"Wow, that's awesome. God is good."

"All the time," said Chana.

I laughed. "You guys sound old.

"How do you know Mr. Tobias?"

I wished Teddy would stop asking questions, but he wouldn't be Teddy if he didn't. "I met him at the hospital and I-I want to check in on him."

Teddy stopped in front of a house. "Well, this is it."

We all stared at the front of the white house with black shutters. It was a boxy house with a driveway on the right side, and it had a very small front and side porch. Shrubs were planted on either side of the porches, as if placed there to break your fall if you fell off, since there were no railings.

"Are you going to go and knock on the door?" asked Teddy.

"Yeah, uh-huh," I replied, but I didn't move.

Chana jumped off her bike. "Come on." She grabbed my hand and pulled me to the door.

"I'll wait here," said Teddy, already back to playing a game on his phone.

Chana raised her hand, and I pushed it down. "Don't ring the doorbell."

"Then how will he know we're here? You're acting really weird."

I wasn't sure I wanted to see Mr. Tobias or hear what he had to say. I wasn't sure about anything anymore.

"Something is talking about coming for you. You need answers."

I stared at the ramp attached to the back of the porch. She was right. "Okay, okay," I replied and pushed the little white button next to the door. No one answered. I pushed it again, and we waited.

Chana tried the knob.

"Don't do that."

"It's open."

"Don't go in there," I whispered after she was already stepping in. I pulled her by the back of her sweatshirt, but she hit my hand away.

Did we go back in time? We walked into a kitchen with each wall covered in yellow, floral patterned, wallpaper. It was a clean house, but very old-looking. Old brown cabinets, old white appliances, and furniture from about nineteen-seventy. It was kind of vintage, I guess.

"Mr. Tobias?" Chana called. "There are an insane amount of angel knick-knacks in this house."

"Yeah, really," I replied, picking up a porcelain angel figurine with a broken wing and setting it back down.

"Mr. Tobias?" she called again as we started down the hall to the back rooms after seeing no one was in the living room.

Chana walked in front of me, and I held onto her sleeve, walking maybe a little too close behind her.

The hall was dark, but the door to one of the back rooms was open, and light spilled in through slats of a blind from a window on the back wall.

Chana pushed me forward. "Go in there. Is that him? I think he's dead."

10

"What's taking you guys so long? I thought someone may have locked you in the basement or something," Teddy exclaimed.

"Shh…"

"Mr. Tobias?" I called.

A grey head of hair turned toward the door. He lifted his face and opened his eyes. "What?" He rubbed his eyes with thick, wrinkled fingers. "Do I know you?"

"We met at the hospital."

"Heyyyyyy…," he said, looking at Chana. "You've come to my house?"

He can't tell us apart? "No, I—me. *I* met you. You said we're special, you and I."

"How are you special?" Teddy whispered.

"Shush."

"Come on. Let them talk." Chana pushed Teddy back toward the kitchen.

"Wait, I want to hear this."

"It has nothing to do with us."

"I don't know what you're talking about," said Mr. Tobias.

"But I talked to you. Don't you remember me?"

He grumbled and groaned as he adjusted himself on the daybed.

A door swung open in the hallway and a woman emerged. "Where did you guys come from?" She held a clothes basket. She'd come up from the basement and looked back and forth at Chana and Teddy in the kitchen and me at the doorway of the back bedroom.

"Are you his grandchildren? I'm his nurse, Paige." She walked toward the room. "You have company," she sang with delight. "Finally. You're alone far too much."

"Don't listen to her. I'm never alone."

"Yes, you are and that's why you're so grumpy."

"He doesn't remember me."

"Really? Don't worry. It'll come back to him. He forgets things sometimes, don't ya, Mr. T.?"

"How did they get in my house? Get them little buggers out of my house."

I took a step back. He looked exactly like the man from the hospital, but with a totally different demeanor.

"Don't be alarmed, he's all bark. He's calmer in the afternoons. It's catheter time anyway, and that's only going to make him meaner for a bit. Do you know what that is?"

"No."

"What's your name?"

"Sheena."

Mr. Tobias looked up at me and turned away, scowling.

"Well, Sheena, I don't want to be the one to break it to you, so look it up."

She ushered me toward the kitchen with Chana and Teddy.

"But…"

"It's hard enough to get him to do it when it's just us here. Come back later."

"But, Mr. Tobias!" I yelled. "Just answer one question for me…"

The door closed behind us.

"Give him a couple of hours," Nurse Paige instructed through the window of the door.

I stood in disbelief and disappointment, staring at the bare mulberry branches hanging over his fence. I knew them well. My Nana had several of the trees in her yard.

"I can't believe she just kicked us out. Who does that?"

"It's okay, Sheena. We'll come back," Chana insisted.

"No, I won't be coming back here. Maybe I was right about him."

"Meaning?"

"He has dementia."

"Maybe so. What did you want to ask him?" asked Chana. "Was it about—"

I shot her a look for her not to say anything. I knew she was about to mention the text message.

"No. I was going to ask about something else. If they can—" I looked at Teddy and then back at Chana and whispered the rest. "If they can take human form."

Teddy looked at me like I was nuts. "Can they take human form? That's right, I heard you. What in the world were you back there talking to him about? No, no, don't walk away. Come back here. Don't pick up that bike." He climbed on his. "I'm just going to follow you, you know. What is going on?"

Chana turned to me. "You might as well tell him." She was right. I'd known Teddy almost as long as I had known Chana. You could say he was my second-best friend, and not future boyfriend.

"Okay, but not here."

"Whose house?"

"Mine," I replied.

We rode fast and didn't say a word all the way there.

"Hey, Theodore, Chana..."

"Mama bear," Chana responded, and gave my mom a hug.

She giggled. "The gang's all here."

"Guys, go on downstairs. I want to check in on my dad. You know the way." My dad sat on the sofa in the sitting area of my parent's bedroom on his laptop.

"How's it going today, Daddy?"

"Just fine, baby girl."

"I'm the only girl."

"So what, you'll always be my baby girl."

"Dad!"

"What?"

I held up the wire hanger next to him. "You are not supposed to be scratching inside your cast with this."

"Have you ever worn a cast?"

"No."

"Then you have no idea what I'm going through. That hanger is worth a million dollars to me right now. Give it back."

"Do you have the money?"

"Sheena…"

"Okay, okay. Chana and Teddy are downstairs. I bet we could wrestle you to the ground like we did as kids, but this time we would win with your broken wing and all."

"Don't let this leg fool you. I can still run through walls."

"Yeah, uh-huh." I kissed him on the cheek, feeling his prickly stubble. The swelling of his face from the accident had gone down, and I could recognize him again. Although his goatee was getting too long, and he was starting to look like a Billy goat, which I had no problem taunting him about.

"Daddy, did you notice anything when you were in the hospital? Anything weird, or that you couldn't explain?"

"Like what?"

"I don't know, anything. Anyone sneaking around or anything?"

"I was knocked out most of the time at first, so I don't know. Why? Do you know of something weird happening?" He looked at me like he knew me—knew what I was thinking.

"Nope. Just wondering. I've heard ghost stories."

"Oh, that's where this is coming from, those old Hackley tales. Nope, nothing at all." He went back to typing. "You know I don't believe in that kind of mumbo-jumbo anyway."

"Yeah, I know. Well, I'll be back to check on you."

"Tell that woman downstairs to bring me a piece of cake, and not the vegan one. I need animal products in my food."

"Ooo... I'm telling you called her 'that woman.'"

"So! I'm not afraid of her. Okay, don't tell her that."

"I'm telling!"

"I have money."

"Ha! You still owe me the million dollars for the hanger."

I ran down the stairs. "Mom, dad wants cake," I yelled as I opened the basement door.

"Cake? Absolutely not. I've got his cake. If he eats this salad, *then* he can have cake. It's like I have another child, trying to get him to eat vegetables."

I laughed as I went downstairs. It was nice having things back to normal, other than my angel issue.

"Finally," Teddy said while grabbing a handful of pretzels from a bowl on top of the pool table.

"Get that bowl off of there before you get me in trouble. Where did you get that?"

"Your mom. Where else? At least she knows how to treat a guest."

"Who's a guest? This has practically been your house since you were, like, seven."

"Okay, well, now that you've graced us with your presence, tell me everything from the beginning and don't leave out anything. I'm talking the full podcast version. And don't lie either. I can tell when you're lying."

Chana leaned over the back of the sofa. "Oh really?" she asked, looking back and forth between us with a huge grin.

I gave her a look that said stop it.

"Yeah, she's really bad at it. She bites her lip and looks off to the side."

"She does, doesn't she?" Chana exclaimed and elbowed him.

"Fine."

I told Teddy the whole story and realized I didn't want to repeat it ever again. It sounded too crazy—just unbelievable. I was glad I had already typed it up and saved it on my tablet.

I watched Teddy and bit down on a nail, waiting for his response.

Chana hit my hand out of my mouth. "Don't do that. You're ruining my hard work." She had polished my nails the night before.

Teddy's brows furrowed as he stared at me without blinking. "You're not lying. You didn't do the lying thing. You really believe this?"

"Yeah, I do."

He turned to Chana. "You too?"

"Yeah, that's my girl. If she says it's true, it's true."

He bounced his fists on the arms of his chair. He was really thinking it through. "So, if you can see angels, which I'm not sure I believe, can you see demons too?"

"We don't know for sure it was an angel."

"If it helped your dad, it had to be an angel."

"Makes sense," said Chana.

"I don't know what else I can see. It only happened that one time. I didn't get to ask Mr. Tobias about it. Maybe it's that one angel in particular."

"Well, I don't think you can count on Mr. Tobias for any information. I think his hamster is dead."

"What? What does a hamster have to do with anything?"

"You've never heard that? The hamster is dead, but the wheel is still turning?"

"No!" Chana and I replied.

"You guys live in a bubble. It means he's cray-cray."

Chana swung at him. "You should have just said that."

Teddy kept throwing out suggestions, and I was glad he was taking it so well. He snapped his fingers. "Go where angels hang out—a church."

"Do you seriously think angels would only be in churches? She just told you she saw one at the hospital," Chana exclaimed.

"Yeah, but at churches you have pastors or priests. You can ask them questions."

"No, I can't do that."

"Just interview one of them like it's a school project. They should be experts on the subject. You're an investigator. Do it."

Chana turned away from the television and toward us, nodding. "You should do it." She turned back and flipped through the channels. "Nothing's on."

"Okay, enough about that before my brain explodes. It's gaming time. Where's the PS4?" asked Teddy.

"Hold on a minute. Someone's calling, or texting."

I took my phone from my back pocket, put in my passcode, swiped up, and glanced at Chana.

"It's him, isn't it? I can see it on your face."

"Who, Mr. Tobias?" asked Teddy.

"No."

"I know you're not saying it's the angel. They use technology? Are you kidding me?"

Teddy jumped up from his seat and snatched the phone from me. "There's no number showing where the text came from. It's just blank, like it came out of thin air. That's impossible."

Chana stepped to his side and read the text aloud. "Seek, and you will find; knock, and it will be opened to you. Hackley Park. Third Street. The tenth hour."

11

"*I*s that a riddle?" asked Teddy.

"Seek, and you will find; knock, and it will be opened to you? It's talking about answers to what you're looking for. Don't you think?" asked Chana.

"Yeah," was all I could respond. I began to feel anxious. Instead of the usual thump-pause-thump-pause of my heart, the beat was a steady and fast thump-thump-thump-thump-thump. This was really happening.

I walked away, leaving the phone with Chana and Teddy. I wasn't sure I wanted to know anything else, but this thing was pushing me toward it. And then I did want to know—to solve this great mystery of what I'd seen and why. But I kept going back and forth between fear and courage and then lingering somewhere between the two.

I spun around. "The tenth hour? It's already past ten."

"No, that's not what it means," said Chana while staring at her phone. "It doesn't mean ten in the morning. Hold on a sec, I'm looking it up. Here it is. It's Jewish time from the biblical days. The tenth hour is four-to-five pm."

"You're not going," Teddy said as he tossed my phone on the sofa and sat down in front of the television. He grabbed one of the gaming controllers, set on moving on from discussing the text.

I gave Teddy a side glance.

"No, you are not. I'm with him," said Chana. "How do you know that's the angel? And I don't understand why an angel uses a phone to communicate when you've already seen him."

"I don't know. Maybe because you're always around me lately."

"You must mean more than usual, because she's always been around," said Teddy.

"You better be glad I'm around. I keep you out of trouble."

"Well, this is more info than the first text."

"The first? Are you saying he's contacted you before?" asked Teddy.

"Oops, did I leave that part out?"

"Yes, you did."

"I didn't respond to the first one. I was scared."

"She was," Chana agreed, as if *she* wasn't.

"You were there?"

"Yep. Can we start the game already?"

Teddy put his controller down. "No. Not until she assures me she's not going."

"Who are you, my dad?" I whispered.

"Don't worry. If she goes, I'm going too," said Chana.

"Great. Then you'll both get kidnapped. You're not going."

"Yes, I am."

Teddy rose from the sofa and stepped in front of my face. "Then I'm going too."

"No, you're not." We were nose to nose. He's taller than me, so not really nose to nose. Maybe his nose to my forehead. Anyway, I could feel his hot pretzel breath in my face.

"I'm going, or I tell your dad you've been texting back and forth with some grown man."

"You wouldn't!"

"You want to find out?"

We stood there for a moment, glaring at each other. Then Teddy walked around me and headed up the stairs.

"You better stop him," said Chana.

"Okay, okay. Come back."

Teddy turned around.

"I'm tired of arguing about this. Fine, you're both going, just give us some space. He may not appear if he sees me with people."

"It's not like anyone but you will be able to see him!" Teddy exclaimed.

Teddy led the way up Fourth Street toward downtown. A ten-minute bike ride to the Hackley Park, turned into twenty, because Teddy demanded to stop for an Oreo shake on the way, claiming he needed nourishment in case he needed to "handle somebody." Yeah, he was tall for a thirteen-year-old, but he wasn't going to handle anyone. He would run just like Chana and me.

"You just think a sugar rush will help you run faster."

Chana didn't laugh at my joke, and we always laughed at each other's jokes, whether they were funny or not. In fact, she didn't say much at all. She mostly rode behind, watching us. I think she was really worried about what was going to happen. At least we were going to a public place, so if anything happened, someone would see and perhaps come to our rescue.

My heart raced with anticipation and a splash of fear as we stopped at the edge of the park.

"Do you see anything?" asked Teddy.

I took in everything—the lawn, walkways, trees, and benches. "No, nothing resembling what I saw at the hospital."

"Your voice is shaking."

"*I'm* shaking. I can't breathe."

"Hold on. This is no time to have anxiety issues. You are the one that dragged us out here," said Chana.

"Dragged you? You demanded that you come."

Teddy pointed. "You two need to stop fussing and pay attention to your surroundings. Look at the trees back there. The branches. They're moving."

"Stop making up stuff to scare us."

I wasn't falling for one of his tricks. There was no way he was going to get me to turn around just so he could laugh and call me gullible.

But the expression on Teddy's face as he watched the trees forced us to turn around. The trees to the right of us had been planted in a straight row down the walk, which was the length of two blocks.

"That's the wind, right?"

"Wind doesn't blow one tree at a time."

The branches of the tree furthest away from us were moving high at the top, and then the one in front of that one, and then faster from one tree to the next, coming closer until it stopped two trees away from us.

We all gasped.

As we waited for what seemed an eternity, branches of the tree twitched as if shivering.

"What is happening?" whispered Chana.

I shook my head but didn't take my eyes off the trees.

Just as she finished speaking, two squirrels jumped out of the tree.

Teddy screamed and then burst with laughter.

The squirrels into the next tree, chasing each other.

"That wasn't funny."

"So not funny," I said as I held my chest trying to slow my racing heart.

"Chill, Theodore. Sheena, we'll wait here, and you ride over past the soldier's monument. See if you see anything."

"That's too far. If someone snatches her, we're too far away to rescue her."

"What are you going to do, anyway?"

"Don't worry about it, I'll handle it."

"We'll ride up a little every few feet."

"Okay, as long as you stay out of the open."

"You just make sure you stay *in* the open where we can see you."

"Uh, this park is completely open."

My throat was suddenly dry. I swallowed hard, staring at the monument at the center of the park. What if one of the four Civil War veteran statues came to life and stepped down from the monument? Based on everything I'd seen lately, it could happen.

I got off my bike, turned back to my friends, and put my hands up as to say, it's okay. I needed to walk. It helped with the anxiety.

When I'd almost reached the Third Street end of the park, I stopped and looked around. I could still see Teddy and Chana back behind me, off their bikes and stooping behind a tree, watching.

"Looking for someone?"

I looked at the empty bench to the right of me and then to the old man in a powered wheelchair to the left of me.

"Mr. Tobias?" *This town is too small.*

"It's about time you arrived."

"It is?"

"Exactly what is it that you want?"

I looked down at the wrinkled hands covered in brown spots, which rested on the arms of his wheelchair. "...To ask you some questions."

"About?"

"You know, you were a lot nicer at the hospital." I looked over his head, around the park. If Mr. Tobias didn't leave, the angel might not show up. What the heck was he doing there anyway?

"What time do you have?"

I checked my cell phone in case I missed an additional text and noticed the other texts were gone. "Four-thirty."

Mr. Tobias leaned forward and looked down the street. "It's within the tenth hour," he mumbled to himself.

"What did you just say?"

He looked up at me. "It's within the tenth hour."

"Why did you say that? Did you text me? Was it you?"

"Text *you?* Do I strike you as the kind of person that texts? I received a text to come here. I thought you just happened to be here."

"A text from who?" I asked.

"I don't know."

"Then why did you come?"

"The language of the text..."

We stared at each other in silence.

"Sit down," he instructed and watched as I let down the kickstand on my bike. "I remember you from the hospital."

I felt relieved. "You do? I thought maybe you needed glasses or something."

"I only need glasses when I'm reading. Other than that, I can look through muddy water and spot dry land."

I almost laughed—almost. My stomach was still turning backflips from anxiety.

"There is not much I will say in front of others. I have to guard the gift. There is warfare going on that you cannot begin to comprehend—yet."

"The gift? Wait, how did you get here?"

"Bus."

"Really?"

"I use a wheelchair, but that doesn't mean I'm immobile." He pointed. Nurse Paige waved at us from several feet away.

"Now, Little Gleamer—"

"I'm not exactly little. I'm thirteen."

"Excuse me. I guess you're practically an adult," he replied with a smirk.

"That's right, I am. Why do you call me 'Gleamer?'"

"You saw what I saw that night, didn't you?"

"I think so. I mean, if you saw a giant, glowing being."

Mr. Tobias nodded. "You have been given a gift. The ability to see things in another realm."

"Well, that explains it, then." I laughed. "No, seriously..."

"Do I strike you as a man that jokes about things?"

"You mean I can see, like, another world happening around us?"

"Is that so unbelievable, based on what you saw?"

I shrugged.

"Tell me what took place at the hospital. How did you happen to be there?"

"My father had been in an accident," I replied and went on to tell Mr. Tobias everything that happened.

He raised his head, looking me in the eye. His eyes still held that spark, like there was a battery behind them making them glow brighter green. His brows rose and fell as he rubbed his chin.

"There's something special about you."

"Me? No, there's not."

"An Archangel revealed himself to you."

"An Archangel? Are you sure?"

"Positive. Think. Was that the first time you've seen anything like that?"

"Yes."

He shook his head. "I doubt it. You may not remember, but your gift probably showed years ago before you could express what you were seeing. Ask your parents."

"Ask them what? Have I seen angels before?"

"No, ask them if you ever had imaginary friends."

12

I think Mr. Tobias came to the same conclusion as I. Someone wanted us to meet up that afternoon. Whatever information I needed was to come from Mr. Tobias. Maybe I could relax now and stop worrying that something was coming for me and would beam me up into space or to another dimension.

"Can you always see them?" I asked Mr. Tobias.

"No, sometimes I know they're around because of a smell."

"Really? What kind of smell?"

"Flowers. Or a feather floats down in front of me, or I witness something that shouldn't be possible, and I know they're near."

"What do you mean by something that shouldn't be possible?"

"People getting healed, something like that."

"Like my dad."

"Yes." He motioned to Nurse Paige and pointed down the road. "My bus is coming and so are your friends."

"But you said that before looking around. How did you know that?"

"I just know. Listen, I won't talk about this around anyone. You will learn what people think of you if you start telling them everything you see."

"But I have more questions about all of this."

"I'm sure you do," he said, sitting up. "Too much information at one time is useless. You will only focus on certain aspects of what I've told you. Your gift is limited right now, and there's a reason for that. A little at a time, Little Gleamer. We'll discuss this further later. They're bringing us together for that purpose."

"They? Are there many? Are they only in the hospital? Is it possible for me to see them anywhere?"

"Yes, they are many and they are everywhere."

"But the one from the hospital—"

Nurse Paige jogged toward us. "Time to go."

The bus pulled up at the corner and Nurse Paige waved at the driver while fussing at Mr. Tobias to hurry.

"Wait! Just tell me one more thing. Can they take human form?" I yelled.

Theodore pulled up next to me on his bike. "Hey, we're out in the open. I don't think you should be yelling stuff like that."

We watched the bus let down some kind of lift for Mr. Tobias's wheelchair.

"Did either of you hear Mr. Tobias? Did he answer my question?"

"How could anyone hear anything anyone else says over his nurse? She never shuts up, does she?"

We watched the bus pull away.

"Well, that was a short talk, what did he tell you?"

"It wouldn't have been so short if you didn't all of a sudden need a milkshake!"

"My bad, what did he say? He sent the text?"

I shrugged. "He really didn't have time to say much."

"Yeah, but you were talking."

"I didn't learn anything."

"Fine. Don't tell us, then!" Chana exclaimed and turned on her bike toward our neighborhood.

"Chana, wait."

"No, keep it to yourself, if that's how you want to be." She pulled off and I watched the back of her two curly afro puffs bob up and down as she pedaled.

"Now you've made her mad," Teddy said and rode ahead to catch up to her.

"What did I do?"

"You did that face thing. She knows you're lying," he yelled back.

Sheesh!

I turned and faced the park, closed my eyes, and lifted my head as a breeze that hadn't been there earlier blew over my face. My eyes flashed open. Once again, I felt someone near me. I jumped on my bike and hurried to the corner, where Teddy waited.

"Look at you running like a bat out of—"

"Shut it, Teddy."

13

I nstead of splitting up and going to our separate homes, we all rode to my house again. Chana pulled into the driveway first and stood next to her bike, waiting.

"Okay, tell."

"Oh, you aren't mad anymore? We're speaking again, are we?"

She smirked. "Whatever, what did he say? Did he send the text?"

"No. We don't know who sent it to us."

"Us? He received one also?"

"Yep, and it told him to be there the tenth hour."

"Whoa, that's a game-changer. I think someone is watching both of you and wanted you two to talk," said Teddy.

"Yeah, I think we figured that out, smarty."

"So, what did he say?"

"Sheena!"

I turned toward the happy little voice calling my name. Dingy ran toward us. He was an only child like me, and always in my business like he was my little brother or something. He lived next door, but it was the backyard of his house that faced the side of my house. I believe he watched out the back window all day just to see when I might go outside so he could either talk my ear off, harass me, or beg to go wherever I went—as if we didn't spend enough time together already when I babysat.

Dingy ran up holding a Catboy action figure and wearing his usual I-love-everyone-in-the-whole-world expression. I looked down at the red boots he wore often, as if he expected it to snow any day. It did snow in October sometimes in Michigan, but it wouldn't be happening this year. We were experiencing an Indian summer. At this rate, he'd be trick-or-treating in flip flops.

"Sheena! I have something to tell you."

"Tell me later, Dingy. Go home."

"Nope," he cheerfully replied while hopping side-to-side, almost in a dance.

"Dingy, what are you, like, six now?" asked Teddy.

"Seven."

"Shoo, go away," said Chana.

"Wait," Dingy replied, holding up a finger. "My mom fried fish."

He knew how to get me over to his house. His mom was the best cook in the neighborhood, and she'd cook enough food for fifty people at the drop of a hat and invite the whole block over.

"I'll come by later."

Dingy ran away, happy, and Chana turned back to me.

"Come on, finish. What were you saying?"

"Mr. Tobias called me a gleamer, just like in the text, and he's one too."

"A gleamer means you see things no one else can see? Is that what he meant?"

"I guess. He thinks I'm special somehow."

"Sheena!" My mom called from the sunroom. "Is your homework done?"

I looked up, remembering my homework for the weekend. I sure didn't get any of it done at Chana's, not that I had planned to.

My mom must have read the *Oops I forgot* followed by the *No* expression on my face.

"Say goodbye to your friends."

"It's like you're five again," said Chana.

"I know. I'll call you later," I whispered.

As Chana and Teddy turned their bikes, I closed my eyes and lifted my face toward the sun, feeling that breeze I felt at the park. "Teddy, see that Chana gets home safely."

"I don't need him to see me home. What era is this?"

I opened my eyes. I wasn't even sure why I'd just said that.

———◇———

Two hours after Chana and Teddy left, I sat at my desk with a pen in my hand, bent over my notebook, staring out at Dingy's house in thought. I looked over the basketball hoop attached to the garage to the array of windows along the back of the house. If anyone watched me, they would've thought I was taking in every detail of our neighbor's property. I didn't really see any of it. I saw Hackley park, the trees and the monument, and my conversation with Mr. Tobias...

BLERP!

I grabbed my cell phone. Teddy's name was on the screen.

"Hey, Teddy. I hope you're not calling with more ideas—"

"Sheena, turn on the news right now!"

I grabbed the remote and pressed the power button for the small screen on top of my dresser. The first image that came up was footage of an accident scene. Words scrolled across the bottom, and a reporter was speaking, but I ignored her as I stepped closer to the television.

No, it can't be! There was a woman holding another woman, crying. The same women from the vision or dream or whatever it was I'd had at Chana's. "Teddy, what happened? Is that Chana's street?"

"Remember you said to see that she gets home safely? Well, I did. It made sense because her street is before mine. This car was speeding, and another car crossed the intersection. The speeding car didn't stop at the stop sign and slammed into the driver's side of the other car. I had just grabbed Chana's seat, pulling her back from crossing.

What the heck, Sheena? When you said that, did you know something was going to happen?"

"No. I mean, I don't know."

My phone beeped. "That's Chana. I'll call you back."

"Wait. Monday, after school, we're going back to Tobias."

"Are you sure?"

"Absolutely." Teddy hung up without another word.

"Did you see?" Chana asked without saying hello. Her voice sounded almost excited. It must have been the adrenaline.

"Of course, I saw. Teddy called me. What happened?"

"Those cars almost turned me to liverwurst."

"That's not funny."

"Why not? What's wrong?"

"Remember that bad dream I had at your house last night?

"Yeah, the one you lied and said you didn't remember?"

"I did the face thing, huh?"

"Uh, yeah."

"In the dream, I saw this..."

14

I don't know how long my mom had been standing behind me, but when I turned around, she was there in the doorway, watching the news report. If she heard my phone conversation with Chana, she didn't show it. I'm sure my expression looked like I'd been caught doing something I wasn't supposed to be doing, like the four-year-old me caught drawing on the wall with a marker. "Set your clock. We're leaving early tomorrow."

That's all she said before closing the door behind her. I stared at the door, but I didn't hear the floor creak. That meant she was still standing there. But why? Thinking? Listening?

I felt bad for keeping things from her, but how do you tell your parents something like this—that you're a gleamer, with no proof and without even knowing what it really is? I didn't want to sound crazy.

I turned back to the news report. This was more than just seeing angels. I saw someone's life.

The next morning, my mom and I sat in the waiting area outside of Pastor Evans' office. The secretary was busying about, getting things ready for the first church service of the day.

I told my mom I wanted to talk to the pastor. She didn't pry about it, but she looked a little concerned.

"Sheena, your nails are polished so nicely. I was so proud you'd stopped biting them, but now you're starting up again."

"That's a nasty habit," we stated, together.

"I know, mom." I put my hand in my lap and focused on the gold glitter specks in the pink polish. I didn't even realize I was biting my nails. I was nervous about talking to the pastor. His eyes could have spiritual x-ray vision. What if he could look right into my soul and see what I've been through, or maybe he could see that glow Mr. Tobias spoke of—if I still had it.

Pastor Evans approached us. His navy suit looked as if it had never seen a wrinkle and his shoes as if they'd never been scuffed. He wore glasses and an expression that said he had more knowledge than anyone in the world. My mom stood to shake his hand. He asked about my dad, and then my mom took it upon herself to tell him I wanted to talk to him about something.

I looked at her with my mouth open. *Really, mom? I can speak for myself. What if I changed my mind?*

"What is it, Sheena?"

"Umm..." I wasn't prepared to talk about it in front of my mom. I hadn't even told her anything yet. She watched me with eyebrows raised. I wondered what *she* thought I wanted to ask him.

How am I supposed to begin? I had rehearsed it in my mirror several times before I left that morning. I thought I'd start with something like, "Pastor Evans, I was wondering about something. There were people in the Bible that saw angels. What about nowadays? Does it still happen?"

I looked at my mom and back at Pastor Evans. I usually had no problem with speaking up about anything, but with my mom there, I'd become mute. The words were jumbled up in my brain and wouldn't come out.

Before I could speak, an usher walked in. "Pastor, Minister Evans is looking for you."

Saved.

"It's probably about communion. Okay, tell my wife I'll be right there," Pastor Evans replied. "Sheena, we can talk between services. Be assured that whatever your question is, if you pray about it, the answer will come, often from the most unexpected place. And don't be surprised if you get the same answer from two or three people to confirm it." He patted my shoulder. "Okay? You'll probably find me by the front doors. Just grab my arm and yank me away from whomever I'm with." He grinned down at me.

I smiled. "Thank you, Pastor."

I didn't talk to Pastor Evans after church. In fact, I avoided him by sliding down to the end of the pew and taking the side exit, steering clear of those that congregated around the main door where Pastor Evans would be.

Outside, I ducked around the building and walked at a quick pace through the parking lot. For the first time ever, I'd be waiting by the car when my mom came out instead of her having to look for me or pull me away from one of my friends.

"Sheena!"

I turned, looking around the parking lot for where the voice came from.

She walked between the next row of cars, toward me.

"Ariel? I didn't see you inside. Are you a member of this church too?"

"No, today was my first time here."

"Did you enjoy service?"

"Yes."

Ariel wore the same jeans and top I'd seen her wear at school and the arms of her jacket were tied around her waist. Always the same outfit.

I looked around. "Where are your parents?"

"At home."

"You came here by yourself?"

"Yep. I wasn't afraid."

"Wow. I don't know if I would have visited a church alone—or wanted to go to one in the first place. You're brave."

"You're brave too. I can see it," she said, looking into my eyes as if she could see a badge of bravery in there.

I looked around Ariel's wavy head of hair, hearing some kids squealing. They jumped around in the grassy area on the other side of the parking lot, as if they were playing a form of hopscotch all at the same time.

"What are they doing?" asked Ariel.

"I don't know. They usually run around until their parents are done talk—"

Ariel headed for the kids.

Okay, sure, just walk off while I'm talking to you just like you do at school. I followed her.

The kids, five-to-eight years old—girls in their Sunday dresses and boys in slacks and collared shirts, stood under a large oak tree looking up. A big black bird chased a smaller bird of the same kind. They flew back and forth over our heads. Then *WOMP!* The smaller bird hit the tree, dropped to the ground, walked a few steps, and flew off again.

"That bird is a bully," one of the kids said of the larger bird.

The birds flew right back to the branches and the chase began again.

"Leave him alone," the kids cried out, while a couple of the boys looked for rocks to throw at it.

We ducked as the birds lowered over us.

"This is crazy. What the heck is wrong with that bird?" I exclaimed.

The smaller bird hit a branch and fell to the ground. It tried to walk and limped a couple of times. The kids surrounded it.

"Back up guys, don't scare it."

We screamed as the bird came flying down at our heads trying to get to the smaller bird.

"Get away," Ariel yelled as she ran forward, swinging her jacket at the larger bird until it flew away. The injured one didn't move. Ariel knelt beside it and spoke softly. "It's okay. I'm not going to hurt you." She reached forward and grabbed the bird.

Her back was to me. *Eww...don't touch that,* I thought. It looked like she blew on it or spoke to it or something.

Ariel put the bird down. It hopped a few steps and turned and looked in her direction, as if to say thank you before it flew away.

"It's all better!" the kids screamed. We watched it lift higher into the air than it had before and fly away from the church.

Wait, what just happened? "Ariel, what did you do?"

"Nothing. It was terrified of the other bird. I just told him he would be okay. The other bird had been harassing him since he found its nest."

She just called the bird a him. How could she know that?
"Are you saying it told you that?"

"Yep."

I began to laugh but choked it back. Ariel looked serious. I wasn't even sure what to say in response.

"I'd better get home. I'll see you tomorrow at school."

"Okay," I slowly replied.

"Sheena!"

"Coming!" I yelled toward the parking lot at my mom.

What is happening to my world, I thought as I ran toward our car. *Am I living a movie right now? No, I've been transported to some kind of parallel universe. That's it.*

I sat in the passenger seat, fastened my seatbelt, and looked over at my mom.

"What's wrong?"

"Do you believe in parallel universes?"

"Sheena, don't start."

15

*M*onday couldn't arrive soon enough, and the school day couldn't pass fast enough. I didn't mind any of the things that usually irritated me about school, like my classmates, an overload of homework as if my teachers didn't know I had homework in other classes, and a certain teacher that clearly didn't appreciate me having a mind of my own. He knew I wasn't one to just accept anything you told me. I raised my hand and noticed a glimpse of irritation on his face before I even opened my mouth to oppose his view.

I didn't hold it against him though. I just gave him my full opinion on why, in this day and time, a city in Michigan, only about two hours from us, should not have to drink contaminated water.

It sparked enough of a debate that most of the class got involved, and the talk took up the whole period. I was glad to not sit strumming my fingers on the desk, waiting for the clock to strike three.

The bell rang. I grabbed my things and rushed to my locker, shoved my books onto the top shelf, grabbed my backpack, and pushed past a group of FPS that didn't want to move out of the way. It was like they thought they owned the hallway or something.

I had to move quickly before my friends found me. Going back to Mr. Tobias was something I needed to do alone, so I didn't tell Chana, and I didn't remind Teddy. I was supposed to go to my graphic design class—part of the after-school program. It just so happened, that class was near the gym, and the back door of the gym led to the back of the school grounds, which was the closest door to Mr. Tobias's street.

The key was to slip past Mr. Prewitt without being noticed. Thank goodness for middle schoolers who were already the size of high school linebackers.

"I'm not doing it, Sheena," said Justin, a member of the sporty group. Football was his life. He was nice, and so funny. But there was only one thing that would get him to help me out. Food.

"Lunch. All next week. You know how much you like my subs. Deal?"

"Dessert too."

We bumped fists. I followed Justin, at an angle where my body could hide behind his.

"Mr. Prewitt is at the door," He whispered, blocking me from his view. "Get ready. I'm going to step in front of him.

"Hey, Mr. Prewitt, I have a question about..."

That's all I heard of their conversation as Justin led him into the class. I dashed to the gym and out the back door.

As soon as I got to the corner of the building, I heard the pap-pap-pap of feet running on the sidewalk behind me.

"Where are you sneaking off to?"

I looked straight ahead and kept walking.

"I told you, you're not doing this alone. There's safety in numbers."

"Teddy, I'm not in any danger. He's an old man."

"Tell that to the women that were chained in that basement by an old man."

"You're making that up."

"No, I'm not. You have to be careful, Sheena. I'm serious."

I smiled to myself, listening to Teddy sound like my big brother. It was nice to know he cared so much. I didn't argue any further. Okay, I'll say it. I was glad he was there—just in case.

We quickly approached Mr. Tobias's house.

"Now, before you start with your fifty-million questions, let him talk. Let's see what he knows," Teddy said as we waited for someone to answer the door.

"Welcome back," said Nurse Paige. "Go on in. He's right there in the living room. I'll be in the next room if you need me."

Mr. Tobias's eyes perked up seeing me come around the corner.

"Hello, again."

I lifted a hand. "Hi."

"Would you like something to eat or drink, like an after-school snack?"

"Yeah—" began Teddy.

I cut him off. "No, we're fine."

"You're missing one of your trio," Mr. Tobias replied, looking at Teddy. "Do your parents know where you are?"

"Umm…Well…"

Teddy jabbed me with his elbow. "I don't like that he's asking that," he whispered.

"You don't have to be afraid of me, kids. Young man, perhaps you should wait in the kitchen."

"I'm not going anywhere."

I was surprised by Teddy's harsh tone.

"You can say whatever you need to say, Mr. Tobias. He knows everything."

Mr. Tobias sighed. "Alright then. Knowing everything isn't always a good thing."

Teddy and I glanced at each other.

"I've given this some thought—how we were both sent to the park that day. I get the feeling I'm supposed to help educate you on who you are, and what you can do." He paused as if he were waiting for me to say something. "Let's start with your questions."

Teddy shook his head, but I ignored him.

"Where is your family? Your nurse says you never have visitors."

"Stop getting personal," whispered Teddy.

"I have two sons, total opposites. The older of the two is a physician in Ohio, and the younger...He...I don't know where he is. He didn't want anything to do with this life of mine. God help him."

Mr. Tobias was silent for a moment, deep in thought. I felt sorry for him and wished I hadn't brought it up, seeing the sadness on his face. I sure wouldn't want my Nana to be alone like that.

I thought it best to change the subject and get back to what I was there for. "Can you tell me about being a gleamer?"

Mr. Tobias cleared his throat. "We're like seers, but we reflect light, and in that brief gleam, we can see what is to come, or what has passed. As I've told you, you're something special. You've been given the ability to see things in the spirit realm."

"Can others see besides you and me?"

"Yes, but not like long ago. There was a time when there were many of us. Man no longer believes, so they can't see or hear the way they used to. That's where you and I come in. We are Type-one gleamers."

"What's that?"

"What's a Type-one?" Teddy asked at the same time.

"What we have is stronger or superior. We sense things and can see things just as clear as you can see me sitting across from you."

"I can't."

"You will."

Teddy placed his hand on my knee. My legs were shaking without me realizing it.

"Is that why the Archangel showed himself? So I would begin seeing things?"

"No, I believe you've come of age."

"What is it for—this gleam or sight?" asked Teddy.

I looked at him as to say, *Why are you asking questions?*

"For you to help. You have to mature—strengthen—"

"Help what or who?" I asked.

"You'll know."

"That's what you've done?"

"Something like that. I have a feeling you will have far greater experiences than I've had and see greater things than I've seen."

It all sounded well and good, but I wasn't convinced. "Well—"

"I can see you need more proof. I want to show you something that will speed this process up a bit."

We looked around the room, expecting to see something. "What?"

Mr. Tobias leaned forward in his seat and lowered his voice more than he already had. "Get to Hackley tonight."

"The hospital?" I whispered.

"Yes."

"How am I supposed to do that?"

"I don't know. Be creative, figure it out."

I looked at Teddy. He shook his head. I expected Mr. Tobias to say something more, but he didn't.

"Let's go," whispered Teddy.

We stood to leave. "Okay, I guess we'll see you later?"

"May your vision be true, Little Gleamer."

Whatever that means.

Once we were outside, I turned to Teddy. "You said *we'll* see you later. What do you mean, we?"

"You already know, if you're going, I'm going."

"But how am I supposed to get out of the house? My parents will kill me!"

Ting! Ting!

I jumped out of my bed, already dressed, and ran to my window, hearing the pebbles hit it. I looked down at Teddy and put my finger to my lips.

"Hurry up," he mouthed.

My heart pounded hard in my chest as I tiptoed to the stairs. I could hear the television on in my parents' bedroom. That should keep them from hearing the door chime when I opened it. Our stupid original wooden stairs creaked with each step, causing me to almost have a heart attack. At the bottom, I waited. Hearing no movement from upstairs, I carefully walked to the back of the house, making sure my mom hadn't fallen asleep on the sofa in the family room. If she had, there would be no way out.

All the lights were off, but I knew the layout of my house, and ran my hand over the kitchen island and then the bar stools as I approached the family room.

I held my breath. Someone was on the sofa.

I walked around the sectional and leaned over the figure. It took everything in me to pull out my phone and shine it slightly toward the figure. Thank goodness it was only pillows and throw blankets.

I went to the back door, punched in the code to turn the alarm off and opened the door. *Ding!* The door chimed. I closed the door behind me and waited. No one came. *One more door*, I thought as I walked through the mudroom. I looked back behind me through the glass top of the door, and thought I saw movement in the hall next to the kitchen. I froze and held my breath. My eyes were playing tricks on me. There was no way I could possibly see anything in the dark. I stepped out of the back door and began breathing again.

Teddy stood with his bike, waiting. I held a finger to my lips, and we walked our bikes down to the corner. "You did that like a pro. That wasn't your first time, was it?"

"I plead the fifth."

"Why are we waiting?" Teddy asked when I stopped and leaned my bike against the street light pole.

"Chana isn't here yet."

"She's not coming. She can't get out."

"Really?" I sucked in air. It didn't feel right having an adventure without her. "Alright. Let's get going then. The sooner we get there and see what's up with Mr. Tobias, the sooner we can get back."

———◇———

The whole ride to the hospital, all I could think was the police were going to see us and pull us over, or the house would catch fire, or there would be some emergency that would make my parents go to my room to get me. I'd done my best to make my pillows and stuffed animals look like me under the blankets. We just needed to hurry.

"We're here," said Teddy as we pulled up to the front of the hospital.

"No, really? Am I blind or something?"

"Dang, bite my head off already. I'm just saying."

"Aren't you going to lock up your bike?"

"At this time of night? Nah, just put it against the rack. No one's out here."

"Boy, if my bike gets stolen and I have to walk home—"

"Okay, chain it then."

I didn't. I watched Teddy and leaned my bike against the rack like he did.

Sliding glass doors parted, allowing us to enter the building.

It must have been a slow night for injuries or illnesses, because there were only two people waiting in the emergency area.

Teddy pointed without saying anything.

Mr. Tobias sat before a woman at the counter. "There they are! They're with me," he announced, waving us over.

"These are your grandchildren?"

He nodded. "What? Is there a problem? Can I not have black grandchildren?"

"No-no-no. That's not what I'm saying. I was caught off guard."

"I'm black too you know. My complexion is very light. What, is this a brown paper bag hospital now?"

She looked down, her face turning red. "Sir, I really don't know what that means, but that's not what I meant." She looked up at me. "Your grandfather wouldn't allow us to take him back until you arrived. Where are your parents? Did you come here alone at this time of night?"

My eyes widened. I hadn't thought about that part.

"Parking the car," Teddy answered for me.

I squatted alongside Mr. Tobias. "Are you alright? How long have you been waiting?"

"Too long," the woman responded under her breath as she placed an identification bracelet on Mr. Tobias's arm. "We could've run tests, so we'd have a diagnosis by the time you arrived, but your grandfather refused."

"I'm fine, dear," said Mr. Tobias, playing along.

"This way, please," she instructed as she walked around the desk and wheeled Mr. Tobias through double doors behind her to her left and into a room separated by curtains. "Stay here for a moment, please."

Mr. Tobias watched her and held a finger up. "Now!"

"Now?"

He looked up at Teddy. "Push!"

I pulled the curtain back to make sure the corridor was empty.

Teddy jumped behind Mr. Tobias's wheelchair and we took off down the hall.

"Where are we going?"

"Back there. Those elevators," Mr. Tobias pointed.

I pushed the button for the elevator and kept pushing, trying to hurry it.

"That doesn't work, you know?" said Teddy, looking behind us to see if anyone was coming. "You only need to push it once."

The doors opened and we rushed in. "What floor?" I asked.

"Tonight…Let's try the sixth."

Did he just randomly pick a floor? Why the heck did I sneak out of my house? I shot Teddy a frustrated look, but he ignored me.

"You really know your way around this place," said Teddy. "What's on the sixth floor?"

"NICU."

"What's that?"

"Intensive care for infants."

The elevator door slid open. We stood in a small lounge area, no larger than a hall, that was blocked off by locked double doors with a rectangular glass pane in each.

"They're not going to let us back there. These areas have more security so someone can't just walk off with a baby," I said.

"We don't need to go beyond those doors. We just need to be on this floor.

"Sheena, look through those windows," Mr. Tobias instructed.

I slowly stepped forward, not knowing what he expected me to see. Nurses walking or holding babies or something? Parents crying over sick babies?

"Am I looking for something in particular?" I asked as I looked through the small glass panel in one of the doors.

Mr. Tobias shook his head. "You're not seeing because you don't want to see."

I'm not seeing, because there's nothing there, I thought. I tried my best to focus, but I really had to pee. I must've stood there ten minutes waiting for something miraculous to happen, but it didn't.

Finally, I figured if I called out what I saw, he would see that I was trying.

"I see a nurses' station, and there's a baby being pushed in an incubator or something. That's it."

Mr. Tobias didn't respond.

"I think he dozed off," said Teddy.

"Because I'm old? I can close my eyes and not be asleep, you know?" Mr. Tobias hissed.

"I still don't see anything."

"You're not at peace. You're uptight, nervous, and I think a little fearful. As long as you stay in that place, you won't see. Your only sight will come from dreams, when your mind has calmed."

"You know I've had dreams?"

He didn't say it, but his expression asked, "Really?"

"Oh, yeah, I guess you would know what I'm going through."

"You're blocking yourself—limiting your vision. There is a deeper reality than what is. Close your eyes and concentrate. Open your eyes with an awareness of what is really happening around you."

I looked back through the window, closed my eyes, inhaled deeply, and exhaled. I listened to the sounds in the lounge, just like I had in my dad's hospital room, until I almost felt I could fall asleep standing up. I slowly opened my eyes and gasped.

What I saw was nothing like in my dad's room, but just as miraculous.

"Oh my gosh!"

"What? What do you see?" asked Teddy.

"How many are there?" I asked.

"One for every child," Mr. Tobias responded.

"They're beautiful."

Teddy ran up to me and looked through the glass, expecting to see them also. And just like that, they were gone.

I turned to Mr. Tobias, my eyes wide and eager for more.

He spoke before I could ask anything, as I sat in a chair next to him. "We all have one that is with us always. But what you are not seeing yet are the others that are also around."

"The others?"

"You need to be aware of them because..." He looked over at Teddy.

"What?"

"You're in danger."

I sprung up. "Why would he be in danger? You didn't say anything about this stuff causing danger to anyone before."

"This stuff, as you call it, comes with a price."

"What price? No, you know what? I don't want to know anymore. This was a mistake. I should have kept my mouth shut about what I saw that night and buried it somewhere deep where I'd forget it ever happened. I should never have sought you out. I shouldn't have snuck out and come here. And Teddy, you shouldn't have come with me. I should be in my bed right now, asleep, just like Chana is."

"I want to know," said Teddy, very serious now. "How am I in danger?"

Mr. Tobias shifted his weight in the wheelchair. "You are in danger because of her. Once the Murk know she's a gleamer, and that she knows what she is, they will want to stop her, but there is a hedge of protection around her for her calling."

"The Murk? What the heck is that, and how does that involve me?"

"The Murk will stress, torment, and cause her any pain they possibly can so she cannot use her gift, or so she'll renounce it." Mr. Tobias's voice became somber. "Since they can't get to her, they'll attack those she cares about."

"No! I don't want this. I don't want some Murk or whatever you're talking about coming after people. How can I make it go away? You can be the last gleamer."

Mr. Tobias turned to me. He looked pained. "You still don't understand that you have a great responsibility. But you've been talking. The Murk don't know what's in your mind, but what you let come out of your mouth tells them everything. I suppose now they are trying to decide what exactly you are."

"I don't even know what exactly I am." I pushed the button for the elevator. "We're leaving."

"Sheena, you need to listen to everything he's saying."

"I've heard enough. He said my friends and my family are in danger." I turned to Mr. Tobias. "What about you? You're my friend, aren't you? Are you in danger also, or do you have this same protection that I have?"

Teddy pushed Mr. Tobias into the elevator. I stared down at him, waiting for an answer that never came.

"And you didn't answer my question the other day."

"You're not ready for any further answers. I misjudged you. I thought you were ready. I thought you were stronger."

Why was he saying that? I felt so confused. I needed to get out of there.

"Leave me right here. They'll find me," Mr. Tobias instructed once we were on the ground floor again.

"We can't do that," said Teddy. "Sheena, wait!"

I walked away, heading for the exit.

"Go with her," I heard Mr. Tobias say. I looked back and saw him whisper something to Teddy.

Teddy nodded and jogged after me. "Sheena, wait up!"

The emergency room staff saw us as soon as we exited the double doors. "Are those the kids?" someone asked.

We ran through the exit to our bikes—thank God they were still there—and took off.

A couple blocks away, I stopped pedaling and looked around.

"What's wrong?"

"I feel like we're being watched."

"By who? By them, the Murk?"

"I don't know. I don't even want to know what the Murk is. Aren't you scared?"

"No."

"You're not scared because this isn't happening to you." I began to tear up.

Teddy placed his hand on my back. "It's going to be okay. We're all going to be okay. If anything is going to happen, you'll somehow see it first and warn us just like you did with Chana."

"But what if I don't see it?"

"You will, but right now you have to calm down. We can't stand out here at this time of night, waiting for the police to drive by. Then you'll have much more to worry about than the Murk. Let's get going."

I sniffed and wiped my eyes. "What did Mr. Tobias whisper to you?"

Teddy looked away. "Something that may help."

16

*I*t was a miracle I made it back in the house without my parents knowing I was gone. I lay in bed pulling long strands of curls apart, angry, thinking about Teddy. Why wouldn't he tell me what Mr. Tobias whispered to him? I even begged, which I would normally never do.

Did he forget I knew his weakness? Just one spider, that's all I needed. A daddy long-legs even, and I could cause him major distress. He was so terrified of spiders. Maybe that's what I should do. Chana and I could tie him to a chair, I could go out back to the shed and find some spiders—there were tons of them out there—I'd come back with a jar full. I bet I wouldn't even need to let them crawl out of the jar onto his shoulder or lap. He would scream and tell me everything I wanted to know.

"Ugh!" I exclaimed. "I'm no torturer."

For a second, I wondered if the angel could hear my thoughts. Then I felt ashamed. *That wasn't me. I was just angry.* "I didn't mean it," I said aloud. And since I wasn't sure of what the angel could hear, I thought it best to keep my thoughts in check.

Although I thought I'd have trouble falling asleep, I drifted off quickly, and I dreamed. A dream so intense I awoke panting with my heart racing. I sat up catching my breath, then reached over the side of the bed and grabbed a notebook and a gel pen out of my backpack. I needed to write it all down before it all disappeared into the dream abyss.

First, some men stole my dad's round stool he used when working on things in our garage. Neighbors saw it happen, but no one would stop them or get a license plate number, so I went after them. I followed them to a dark building on a campus of some sort.

Inside the building, there was a black sludge, worse on different floors and really bad in the attic. It reminded me of a thick gooey black mold. But it was alive. It covered the stairwells too, rolling and swelling, blocking my exit. I searched and searched for a way out while dodging the sludge tentacles it threw out, barely missing me. Finally, the only way I could escape was to burst through a window.

The sludge was after some kid, but it wouldn't leave that building.

Then the whole scene switched. Dingy, the kid next door, was there for some reason. I promised to take him to see the new Spiderman movie for his birthday, but there was a strange guy there—a friend of his mom's. And he was evil. He was somehow a part of that sludge.

I had to figure out a way to save everyone from him. I stood in between them, looking back and forth from the guy to Dingy, his mom, and the people that were suddenly behind them. Quite a few of them were kids. The guy lunged toward them, but he would have to go through me to get them. I jumped, throwing my body horizontal in front of them to block him off.

I awoke before feeling the impact and sat up squeezing my t-shirt at my chest. *I used my body as a shield,* I thought. *What was that about?* One thing was for sure, I was not going back to sleep any time soon.

My hands searched over my blanket for my phone. No matter what time it was, if Chana wasn't in a deep sleep, she always picked up for me. I typed a text message, deleted it, and sat the phone next to me on the bed. Mr. Tobias's warning about my friends and family kept repeating in my head. I would put them in danger.

***

"Sheena, what's wrong?" my mom asked before I left for school. "You look like you haven't slept a wink."

"Nothing," I replied as a grabbed my lunch from the refrigerator.

I wasn't trying to be a brat. It's just that I had nothing further to say. I couldn't help it. I couldn't act all cheery-jolly when I had so much on my mind.

"I'm making breakfast—"

"No, thank you."

"You need to eat."

"I have granola."

I quickly kissed her on the cheek and headed for the front door. I knew without turning around that she stood there still holding her spatula, staring at me.

As I walked down the front steps, my pocket vibrated. Chana had already called twice that morning and sent several texts. I guess it was about time I answered.

I stopped walking and stared at the screen.

It wasn't Chana.

Gleamer, you are not alone, it read.

My eyes began to water. I didn't realize how overwhelmed I'd become with everything until that first tear rolled down my cheek. Another text followed that one with a phone number.

Before I could talk myself out of it, I tapped the number and it connected, ringing several times before it was picked up by a familiar voice.

"Mr. Tobias?"

"Little Gleamer, how did you— Never mind, I think I already know the answer to that. Have you calmed down?"

I nodded and sniffed as if he could see me. I opened my mouth to speak but nothing came out as tears continued to roll down my cheeks.

Mr. Tobias let out a deep sigh and spoke gently. "Has something happened?"

I tried to speak again, but only whimpered.

"Close your eyes, Little Gleamer."

I stood on the corner and did as he instructed, not even thinking about what I looked like if someone saw me.

"Breathe in and out deeply."

I stopped crying and took a couple of deep breaths.

"Think about whatever is bothering you from beginning to end. Picture it, like a movie."

There was so much, but the dream was the first thing that came to mind. I don't know how long I stood there. I jumped hearing him speak again. I'd forgotten I was on the phone.

"I saw it," Mr. Tobias said. "That sludge from your dream—something's coming and people are in danger."

Had we just connected somehow? How did he do that?

"You're not alone."

That's what was in the text.

"I don't know why you were shown this. You haven't matured enough for this warning. You must be connected to it somehow."

"What kind of warning?" There it was. My voice was back.

"I'm not sure yet. Watch the people around you. There will be signs. I'll get back to you. May your vision be true."

Why does he always say that? True? Like in my dream? Was that a vision? I don't want that to be true. I was pretty much chased by a river of black lava that was alive! I thought as I watched cars passing by.

A guy in a silver truck stopped at the stop sign and glanced over at me.

I gasped.

He quickly turned away and sped off.

Either I'm seeing things. or his eyes just flashed red.

I hurried to school. In homeroom, someone plopped down in the seat next to me. My mind was on that guy's eyes. I believed I'd seen them before.

"Oww!" I rubbed my arm from the jab. "What was that for? You're so violent."

"What do you think it was for?" said Chana. "I've been texting you all morning, and you haven't responded. What happened? Did you get caught? Is that why you didn't text back? Did your parents take your phone? You must be grounded for the rest of the year."

"You haven't talked to Teddy?"

"I haven't seen Theodore. He's not even in class yet."

I looked ahead at the vacant seat where Teddy usually sat in class just before Clarence sat down there.

"It was a mistake. We never should have snuck out."

"What? Why? Did you get more information?"

"Not really."

I tried to change the subject. "Your bun is super cute. I should've worn my hair up—"

"I don't care about that. Did you see anything?"

I thought about what Mr. Tobias said about the Murk not being able to see what's in my mind, but when I talk, they learn all they need to know. "No. It was uneventful." *Don't bite your lip. Don't look off to the side. She knows when you're lying.*

Chana looked at me strangely. There was so much I wish I could tell her. But if I acted like I still didn't know what I was, which I really didn't really, the Murk wouldn't know either. Sheesh, why didn't I calm down enough at the hospital to ask more questions, so I could've at least found out what the Murk were? Now I wouldn't know what it was if I saw it, or them, coming.

The next day, I waited for Teddy to sneak up on me and pull my hair, or punch or poke me when I wasn't looking, or run up on me and Chana with a, "Double trouble! What's up?" But it never came.

As much as Teddy complained about school, in all the years I'd known him, he never missed a day. I believe he held off getting chickenpox until summer so he wouldn't miss school. Where the heck was he?

I texted him that night, but he didn't respond. Chana and I checked his grams and snaps, but there were no new posts.

"Is Theodore sick?" Mr. Haleigha asked in class, like I know all of Teddy's business.

"I don't know."

The last thing I wanted to do was go to his house. Talk about the most irritating parents ever. His mom treated us like babies and his dad made fun of me every chance he got. "Just leave her alone, Dad, please," Teddy would say as his dad laughed at his corny jokes. Being the respectful girl that I am, I faked laughing so his dad would really think he was funny.

I ignored Chana's stares in class. I think she was worried about me even though I tried to assure her that everything was okay. I was totally stressed, though. Mr. Tobias hadn't gotten back to me about the dream, I couldn't figure out why the guy in the truck's eyes flashed red, my mom acted like she thought I might be on drugs because of how distant I'd become, Teddy was missing, and Ariel stopped showing up also. I didn't even know where she lived so I could check on her. Nor did anyone else. I was more than ready to go back to the way things used to be—pre-Tobias—pre-angel sighting.

After a couple of days things were back to normal, like all was becoming right in the universe again.

"Sheena!" Ariel called from the hall as I headed to my class. Her eyes were brighter than any human being I had ever seen, except for one...Mr. Tobias...Her eyes were like Mr. Tobias's. *Interesting.*

Her flowery scent hit me before she got close.

"Ariel, where have you been? Were you sick?"

"No, I had to, umm...go out of town."

"Oh."

She touched my shoulder.

"Ouch."

Her fingers flicked together, releasing the piece of lint she'd removed from my hair. "Sorry, I carry a lot of static electricity. I'm overflowing with energy." She laughed and looked around at the FPS that were prancing down the hall. "You know, not everyone here is as nice as you. Thank you for that. I will remember it forever."

Why did she say that? "Are you going somewhere?"

Instead of replying to my question, she said, "We have gym class together now. Did you know that?"

"No. Were you just added?"

"Yep," she said with a huge grin.

"Okay, after lunch I'll see you there. Where's your next class?"

"Upstairs."

"What subject?"

"I don't know. I know when I get there," she laughed.

I shook my head, watching her bounce away. She was the sweetest, oddest girl I'd ever met. *How does she not know her class?*

"Boom shakalaka!"

I think I jumped ten feet.

"Stop sneaking up on people. Why are you even saying that, did you just dunk a ball or something?"

Teddy couldn't stop laughing. "Nope, just sneaking up on you. You're best friends with the new girl now?"

"No, just friends." I pulled him to the side. "Something is odd about her."

"Ya think?"

"No, I mean really. But we can talk about that later. I stared at Teddy with my I-should-punch-you look.

"What?" asked Teddy.

"Are you going to tell me?"

"Tell you what?"

"Where have you been?"

The bell rang.

"We're late, run!"

Teddy walked into class with a huge grin and his arms outstretched as if he expected the whole class to smile and cheer at his appearance. Instead, he received several laughs and one clap.

He jumped into the seat next to me, causing the girl that was about to sit there to have to find another seat. "Good-bye, see you later," he said as he waved at her.

"That was rude, Teddy. Excuse him," I said to the girl. Chana sat on the other side of me.

"Any new developments? I keep forgetting to ask you about that question you were supposed to ask Mr. Tobias."

"What question?"

Chana leaned toward me and whispered. "Can they take—"

"Oh, no. I forgot. I still need to ask about that."

"Then what the heck did you talk to him about?"

"I don't even remember." I looked ahead at the blackboard, at her from the corner of my eye, and back at the blackboard. *Sheesh, she knows me. She knows I'm keeping something from her. I need to figure out what I'm going to tell her, just a little something that I won't have to go into detail about.*

Chana sucked her teeth. "I have something. I asked my parents about him."

"What did they say?" I wanted to know even though now I totally believed everything Mr. Tobias said about himself.

"My dad said Mr. Tobias used to help the police. He called with information, or he would show up at a crime scene, and they thought he was a part of the crimes that were happening at first. They think he has ESP, or something."

"Chana and Sheena, do either of you have the answer?"

"Ubiquitous!" Chana exclaimed.

The whole class turned to us and laughed.

"He hadn't really asked a question," said Teddy.

"Okay, that's enough. Pay attention, please."

"You got it, Mr. Haleigh," Chana replied.

I turned toward the teacher and sat up straight in my seat. I looked like I was paying attention, but I wasn't. I thought about what Chana's parents had said. *Is that how I'm supposed to help? Am I going to be able to do what Mr. Tobias did and help the police?* I couldn't see myself doing it and didn't want to know about murders and whatever else might be going on. Kids don't know about that kind of stuff. I wanted to stay in my naive little cocoon.

The lights dimmed and the movie version of the book we were reading began to play on the screen at the front of the room.

Chana tried to slip me a note, but my eyes drifted toward the windows.

The sky darkened. It didn't darken like storm clouds had drifted in, but like something large and dark flew past the window, circled around, and hovered near.

I stood transfixed by the shadow and walked to the window.

"Sheena...What are you—?"

I didn't see anything outside, but then I closed my eyes and focused, removing any room noises. I opened my eyes and froze there like a statue. At least I didn't scream or panic.

"Sheena," said Mr. Haleigha.

Teddy jumped up and ran to my side. "She wants to pull down the shade so we can see better," he said as he pulled down the shade of the next window. I know he was covering for me, but I couldn't tear my eyes away from what I saw.

"What are you doing?" Teddy whispered. "Pull down the shade."

I reached up as I stared out the window. "The Murk," I whispered.

"Just pull it down," Teddy responded nervously.

I trembled as I pulled the shade down and then ran from the room.

Down the hall from the class, I leaned forward and braced myself with an arm out against the wall, breathing heavily.

Mr. Tobias was right. I can see them, and they know where I am. But what I was more concerned about was the dark area that swirled and expanded was most severe near Mr. Tobias's house.

Teddy followed me out of the class. "What is it?" he asked.

"Mr. Tobias…" I replied, my eyes tearing. "They're going for him."

"Who?"

"The Murk."

17

"*W*ait right here," Teddy instructed.

I nodded while leaning against the lockers, trying to calm myself to keep from hyperventilating.

He ran back down the hall a few minutes later. "I called Mr. Tobias. He's okay."

"Are you sure?"

"Yeah, but he's worried about you, though. Like you're really his granddaughter or something. He wants us to come over."

"I don't want to. Wait, why do you have his number?"

"He gave it to me. I'm kind of team-Tobias now. I believe him. He says there are things you need to know. He mentioned your dream. What did you dream?"

"I-I don't remember."

"You remember. I can tell. You know, Chana and I are a part of this with you. We stand with you, or we fall with you. That's the kind of friends we are. Don't push us away."

"I'm not."

"Yeah, right. Anyway, about that angel, I know you're scared, but there's some kind of major destiny you have, I think."

"Yeah, but I didn't ask for it. My normal destiny was fine with me. I didn't want to be a gleamer. Things are happening..."

"What things?"

"Nothing."

"There you go again. You're really starting to get on my nerves. Stop shutting me out."

The bell rang, and Teddy and I were still standing in the same place, arguing. I needed to go back in the classroom and make up something to explain myself to Mr. Haleigha.

Kids flooded the hall. Those from my class looked at me like I was more weird than usual.

"I'll meet you in the cafeteria," yelled Chana before hurrying off somewhere.

After I mustered up enough fake tears to make Mr. Haleigha believe I wasn't faking having stomach pains (somewhere between I stubbed my pinky-toe on the bed frame, and my cat died), I grabbed my sack lunch from my locker and trudged to the lunchroom.

Chana walked up, put her arm through mine, and dragged me off to the lunch counter with her. "Rumor has it—meaning bathroom gossip—you ran out of class because you had to throw up. Are you okay? And what were you lovebirds in such an intense conversation about?"

"Kissing."

Chana almost dropped her lunch tray. "Really? Will it be your first kiss?"

"No."

"Dang, how many boys have you kissed?"

"No, I meant I was joking. You know everything about me. You would know if I'd been kissed."

"Just checking, but I bet Teddy kissed you. That's what happened when you ran out of class, huh?"

"*Yeck*, no! Stop it."

"Well, it should happen. You guys need to stop fighting it, you're getting married one day."

I rolled my eyes.

"Anyway, you've been off, but something is even more off about you today," Chana said as she carefully placed french fries inside her cheeseburger. That's the way she always ate burgers and fries, and she was the only person I'd ever seen do it. "Here comes your friend."

I looked up, seeing Ariel approach and sit with us.

"Are you going to eat today?"

"I'm not hungry," she replied, looking around.

"Are you sure? I have extra."

"I'm sure. That kid over there in the jean jacket, he didn't get in the lunch line and he didn't bring a lunch."

She just came in. How could she possibly know that? I pulled a sandwich out of my bag. "Do you want to give it to him?"

"May I?" She asked with a grin.

"Of course."

We all watched her—everyone at the table, I mean.

"She's like a giddy seven year old."

"I know, right?"

The kid took the sandwich from her. She sat down with him and they talked and laughed.

"Wow, okay."

After lunch, Ariel asked for my number. "Thank you. I'll call you. I promise not to drive you crazy."

"Too late," Chana mumbled.

I didn't see Teddy after school. That was on purpose. I avoided the areas where we could possibly run into each other. We'd done enough arguing for the day, and all of his questions were exhausting me.

I texted Chana as I walked along the walkway in front of the school, to see where she was. She didn't respond, so I continued up the block. At the next intersection, Ariel stood across the street, talking to someone in a silver truck.

I thought, *Good. I'm finally going to get to see one of her parents—I think.* She never mentioned them except for her mother giving her that bracelet. For all I knew, she lived with her grandparents, or aunt and uncle.

I stepped up to the curb, trying to peer inside the truck just as Chana ran up behind me.

"Hey, you left me. Theodore is looking for you."

"Good for him."

"Well, you sure have an attitude this afternoon. What are you looking at?"

As she spoke, the guy in the truck turned toward us. I gasped. "It's him!"

"It's who?"

"Ariel, get away from that truck!" I yelled.

I don't know what I thought I was going to do, but I bolted across the street toward her with Chana close on my heels. The truck sped off.

Chana continued on, a few feet ahead of us.

"What are you doing?"

"Getting the license plate number," she yelled.

"What's wrong?" asked Ariel. She looked startled and confused.

"Sheena!" Teddy called from behind us as he ran up the block. "What the heck? You know there are rules to crossing the street, right? Why are you guys out here dodging traffic?"

"What are you even doing on my street?"

I turned back to Ariel. "Why were you talking to that man? Did you know him?"

Chana ran up to us. "I couldn't see all the numbers."

"What happened?" asked Teddy.

Before Ariel could respond, we all looked up hearing tires squeal. The truck made a huge U-turn and raced back toward us, swerving around cars.

"Run!" yelled Chana.

"What? Why are we running?" yelled Teddy.

"He's after us. This way," I exclaimed.

"Why is someone after us?" Teddy yelled as the four of us ran, backpacks flopping on our backs—except for Ariel. I don't think I ever saw her with a backpack. We sprinted between two houses, through a backyard, and out onto the next street over.

"I hear the truck," said Teddy. "Why is someone chasing us?"

"Come on."

We ran up the block toward the school to the crossing guard.

"What's going on?" asked Mr. Putnam as he put his hand out for some younger kids to stay back until he allowed them to cross.

"A guy in a truck came after us."

Mr. Putnam pulled out his radio and called someone for assistance.

I turned looking back behind me. There was no sign of the truck. "Where's Ariel?"

Chana looked around. "I don't know. She was right behind us."

I ran back the way we'd come.

Mr. Putnam yelled for me to stop, but I didn't listen.

I looked into each yard and alongside every house as I sprinted past. I began to panic. *What if he caught her? Some gleamer I am. Why didn't I know this was going to happen if I'm a gleamer?*

I emerged from behind two rows of houses and stepped into the center of an alley, looking both ways. The truck turned into the far end of the alley and sat there, as if we were in a standoff.

I froze in place in my running stance. *What is he going to do?* I thought. I could only hope that an angel was near me or watching. *Wherever you are, I need you here right now. Please, Please, please.* Just maybe the angel could hear my internal cry and intervene on whatever was about to happen.

Time slowed as a light breeze blew curls into my face, partially blocking my sight. My heart pounded wildly.

Fences with sheds or garages behind them lined the alley on either side.

I pushed my hair out of my face. The back of a purple t-shirt and jeans stood in front of me. Ariel was just there—in the middle of the alley between me and the truck. She stood there in a threatening way as if she could take on a truck like King Kong or something.

The truck raced toward us.

"Ariel!" I screamed and dove off to the right. The truck sped past. I rolled over as Chana leaned over me, helping me up. Teddy lay against a fence over Ariel, having rushed out and tackled her, pushing her out of the street.

Chana and I ran over to them as Ariel stood up.

"Are you okay, Sheena?"

"Am I okay? Are *you* okay?"

"Can someone please explain what the heck is going on?" demanded Teddy.

I picked up Ariel's bracelet from the ground. I guess the rope had broken when Teddy dove at her.

"Ariel, look," I said holding it out to her.

Ariel grabbed her arm where the bracelet should have been and then reached for the bracelet. She looked more frightened about that than about the truck.

"Oh no," she said. "I have to go."

She started to run away but turned back. "Thanks, Theodore."

We watched her turn down a side street.

"Wait, he could be waiting down there!"

"He's not! He's gone!" she yelled behind her.

"Yo, that was ridiculous," Chana said, covering her mouth. "I can't believe that just happened."

"Yeah, well it did, and we have to get back to Mr. Putnam. All of this has to be reported to the police."

We turned toward the school. Teddy pulled on the sleeve of my jacket. "Was that the Murk?" he whispered.

"No, but it was someone very bad."

"Is it a coincidence that he was right here on your street?"

I looked at Teddy and stopped walking. I hadn't thought of that.

Chana turned around. "What? What's wrong now?"

18

"$\mathcal{W}$hat a story for the news," my mom said as we pulled into our driveway.

"Mom, it's not going to be on the news."

"You're not, since you refused to be interviewed, and I didn't give permission for them to even use your image, but the story is."

"Now if you looked like me..." she said with her hand up near her head, showing off her burgundy turban headwrap, "... maybe I would have pushed you to."

"Yeah, right. Your wrap looks cool though. You finally learned to do it."

I stood behind her as she unlocked the front door. "Do I have to discuss the whole thing all over again with Dad, and then call Nana as you would normally have me do, or can I go up to my room...and you tell them," I said with a sly grin.

Music and laughter came from the back of the house. I looked back at my mom. "Who's here?"

She shrugged and pushed me forward.

"What's all of this?" I asked as I walked to the kitchen followed by my mother.

Bouquets of pink and blue balloons hung around the room. Dingy ran forward and grabbed my hand, pulling me further into the kitchen where pink, blue, yellow, and green swirls of a unicorn ice cream cake sat on the island looking like a box of pastel crayons exploded.

"You're a hero," sang Dingy, hopping up a couple times in his red boots.

"How am I a hero?"

The adults looked at Dingy as if they weren't sure if they should say anything in front of him. Dingy's mom stood behind him, placed her palms over his ears, and shook her head. "You saved a girl."

Dingy shook his head roughly, tearing from her embrace. "What are you doing?" he asked, looking up at her. "The cake was my idea!" Dingy exclaimed while dancing around it.

I turned to my mom. "I don't feel like it," I whispered.

She gave me that look that said just go along with it.

"Do you like it?" asked Dingy.

"Yep, just what I wanted," I responded with my best fake smile.

"Tell us everything," my dad said.

My mom shook her head while at the same time Dingy's mom responded, "Uh, maybe not. Little ears absorb everything, and it leads to bad dreams. Let's cut the cake."

"Yes, cut the cake already. I've been waiting for a hundred hours!" Dingy exclaimed.

"Shenna, get plates from the pantry."

I turned to the butler's pantry, directly behind me, happy to get away from everyone for a moment, but my mom followed me in.

"This was all Dingy's mom idea. She saw the report and called, worried about you. Your dad told her you were the hero they spoke of. She brought everything over. You know how she is—any excuse for a celebration." She brushed my hair back away from my face. "It'll be over soon."

I sighed. "I guess I *could* use something sweet since all you feed me is grass and twigs."

"Ha! That's my girl."

My mom turned and left the room as I gathered dessert plates and spoons.

"Sheena," Dingy's mom sang a few minutes later.

I rushed into the kitchen with the plates, realizing I'd been standing there for too long, lost in my thoughts.

"Yes?"

I placed the plates on the island and watched her cut the first piece.

Behind her, my mom and dad were laughing and fussing, no doubt about him having sweets. "You need protein, not sugar," my mom said. "Sugar smooths out muscle."

Dingy's mom handed me the slice. The light blue cake and ice cream looked both disgusting and delicious at the same time. "Do you think you can watch Dingy for me tomorrow evening?"

"I have to ask those two," I replied, pointing at my parents. "But it should be okay."

"Don't think I didn't hear you call us 'those two,'" said my dad.

I laughed as I filled my mouth with the perfect ice cream-to-cake ratio.

My dad sat down at the table. "Get me some cake, woman," he exclaimed, and smacked my mom on the bottom.

"You ever had kale chips on your cake?"

"Don't you dare!"

"Try me."

"Dingy, don't let her do it!" My dad yelled.

Dingy was happy to become a part of the game and laughed as he spread his arms out wide, blocking off the refrigerator.

I looked down at my pocket. My phone was vibrating. I contemplated checking it but didn't know if the celebration constituted a family dinner. We had a rule that we couldn't use phones or even check them during dinner.

I decided to take my chances and I slipped out of the room while everyone was laughing and talking.

Texts were coming in back to back.

U have some explaining 2 do!

What happened?

R U OK?

Thanks again, Sheena.

I know that was you they spoke of on the news. We need to talk asap.

Gleamer, you are forgetting an essential part of your journey. You are powerless without it.

I knew without reading the names, who each text came from. Teddy, Chana, Chana, Ariel, Mr. Tobias, and lastly... of course the last text had no origin.

"Sheena?"

I put my phone back in my pocket and spun around.

"You must be exhausted. I'm sorry to intrude on your evening—"

"We're not intruding," said Dingy.

Dingy's mom put a hand over his mouth. "—but I wanted to celebrate your bravery. We're going to head out now."

"Can we take cake with us?"

"No, we can't take cake with us."

"Yes, you can!" my mom yelled.

"But we brought it," said Dingy.

My mom was already cutting a huge hunk for them to take home.

Dingy grabbed the container from my mom. "We need to hurry before it melts." That would be the first time he was every anxious to leave my house. Now I knew what the secret was to get him out of there.

"What do you say?" asked his mother.

"Oh, thank you, Mrs. Meyer."

I walked Dingy and his mom to the front door. It was colder outside than it had been in recent nights. Maybe our Indian summer was coming to an end.

After they'd gone, I continued standing in the door looking around at the trees up the block and noticed how much the leaves were changing. There were more yellow and orange-red leaves now. I loved autumn for this reason. My mom walked up behind me. "Are you going to let all the heat out of the house?"

I shook my head, still watching the trees. "Do you need me to help clean up?"

"I've got it. You go on up and shower...and do your homework."

I sat on the end of my bed in my robe with a towel wrapped around my hair. The smell of barbeque passed gently through the air from outside. I guess my dad decided to fire up the grill. Although it smelled good, I didn't want any.

He was definitely feeling like his old self. I wished my window faced the back of the house so I could watch him in front of my willow. Instead, my room faced the side. It was like back when someone built the house they decided that one day the house beside it would have a little boy that was obsessed with the girl next door, so there had to be a bedroom window facing the back of his house so he could look for her every chance he got.

I stretched my arms out to the sides and fell back onto my bed as if I were falling back into a pool of water, and imagined water filling my ears as I floated on Lake Michigan. A calmness spread over me.

I revisited the events of the day: I had my first glimpse of what I thought was the Murk. We were chased and could've been killed by a strange guy in a truck. *That Ariel!* I was suddenly upset with her and decided her parents need to whoop her gullible little naive butt. It was like she wasn't even aware of the dangers that existed in the world. But the way she appeared in the road to protect me...Then, the way she reacted about her bracelet being broken. She was so upset about that bracelet. I just couldn't figure her out.

I sat up, losing the sense of relaxation I'd just felt. It was all too much. I needed help.

That's it! If I needed help, why wasn't I asking for it. That's what that last text meant. That's what it had to mean.

I went to my window and knelt, resting my arms on the sill, looking up at the stars that were beginning to show themselves. But I wasn't shooting for the stars. I was shooting for beyond the stars, to a place no one else could see but me, and I guess Mr. Tobias.

"This is becoming too much to handle. Please help me. And can I sleep tonight—I mean with no dreams or revelations or anything—just sleep. Just for tonight? Please? Also, can my friends get a peaceful night's rest also? Oh, and that guy, please let the police find him."

I watched the stars. Was there more that I needed to say? I rested my forehead on my arms and closed my eyes. I didn't speak out loud, but within my heart. When I lifted my head, I don't know what I expected. I didn't feel any different or like anyone heard me. But I believed I'd sleep well that night. And I did.

My mom said she came in to check on me, and I was snoring. And it was only eight o'clock at night. I slept right through the night and didn't wake up until the next morning.

When I awoke, I didn't feel like a special gleamer or anything. I just felt like a teenager with stinky breath and white crusty mucus at the corner of her eye. "Thank you," I said aloud as I stretched.

It's going to be a good day, I thought with a smile as my stomach growled louder than I'd ever heard it. The sound was like a meow-moooooo combined with a rumble.

I rushed and got ready for school. As I texted Chana our usual good morning text, that we'd both been slacking on, the smell hit me.

My hero! My mom was making pancakes. I bet she'd heard my stomach all the way from the kitchen.

"The dead has arisen."

"Poor choice of words, Dad," I replied after kissing him on the cheek. He sat at the counter pouring maple syrup over a plateful of silver-dollar pancakes and sausage.

"Mmmm...you're right. Sorry, baby girl."

"I'm dropping you off at school today." My mom said. "And maybe every day until they catch that maniac."

"You don't have to do that, Mom."

"I know I don't. But I'm not taking any chances with your safety."

"He's probably laying low after the story being on the news."

"Ha! Laying low?" I laughed. "I got that from television."

"You may or may not be right about that. What about your friend you were protecting? Does she need a ride?"

"I-I don't know," I said after rolling up a sausage link inside of a pancake, swirling the end in syrup and taking a bite. My eyes rolled back. *This is so good.*

"I don't know where she lives."

"Well text her and find out. I know you have her number."

I studied my sticky fingers, trying to figure out how I could pull out my phone without getting syrup all over it. I settled on washing my hands first, and then texted Ariel, but she didn't respond.

"Maybe she's too shaken about what happened to attend school today."

"You've got a point," my mom replied as she sat a cup of orange juice in front of me. "I know you didn't pack your lunch last night, so pack it between bites. Maybe I can get you to school on time for once."

School was blah that day, but that's not a bad thing. That's a normal day. I looked for Ariel, but she didn't come to school. Teddy gave me the silent treatment all day for not answering his questions, and Chana was, well, like always, my best friend.

I babysat Dingy that evening and we watched his favorite movie while we sat on the floor with all of the superhero action figures that were in the movie so we could simultaneously act out the scenes.

He was so amazed at my ability to act out the parts, and I liked looking like this talented actor in his eyes. But the truth is, Dingy had made me watch the movie so many times that I knew the entire movie by heart.

My movie of a life seemed to be calming down for a bit, and after a couple of days, although I needed the break, I actually missed not talking gleamer business with Mr. Tobias.

Then, everything went left—I mean it flipped before my eyes. One minute I was leaving school and waiting at the corner to cross the street since my mom hadn't arrived to pick me up, and I was going to end up being the last kid there. I was used to her running late, but this was later than usual. The next minute, an ambulance sped past with sirens blaring and lights flashing, heading down the road toward Mr. Tobias's street.

The vision of the Murk flooded my mind. I ran to the next corner toward his house. The ambulance turned right and pulled into Mr. Tobias's driveway.

"Oh, no!"

I waited, pacing back and forth.

A body was brought out on a stretcher.

Something is really wrong this time. I freaked out. *Where is Teddy when I need him?* I bolted in the direction of my house and didn't stop until I arrived and ran up the front steps.

"Mom, I have to go to the hospital."

My mom stood in the foyer, pulling the strap of her handbag over her shoulder. "Sheena, what are you doing home? You're supposed to wait for me at the school."

"Mom, can you take me?" I asked as I began to pull her.

"Wait, hold on. Calm down," said my dad, grabbing me with one hand while the other rested on one of his crutches.

"Sheena, look at me. What's going on? Are you hurt?"

I began to cry. "No. An ambulance—I have to see him—the hospital."

"Him who? Who are you talking about? Is it Theodore?" asked my dad.

"Mr. Tobias."

"Mr. Tobias?"

My parents looked at each other. "Do you know who that is?" My dad asked my mom.

"No. Sheena, how do you know him? Is he a teacher?"

"He's an old man. He lives across from the school and I saw an ambulance take him away after school."

"Okay, okay, calm down. We'll go. Honey, call and see if there is a Mr. Tobias over at Hackley..."

My dad pulled his cell phone from his pocket.

I paced the kitchen, round and round the center island in a panic, waiting.

"Sheena, here, drink some water."

I took a large swallow and held the next mouthful water in my mouth without swallowing.

"They've got him!" my dad exclaimed.

I gulped down the water.

My mom grabbed her keys, "Okay, let's go."

My mom kept glancing over at me in the car. I snuck a peek at the speedometer. Why did it seem like we were driving too slow? I wanted to slam my foot down on top of her foot on the gas pedal, so we'd go faster. And why was every traffic light we approached red at a time like this?

We finally pulled in front of the emergency room entrance and I jumped out of the car before it came to a stop.

"Sheena!" my mom screamed.

I ran inside to the emergency room counter. My mom must've left the car where it was, because I could hear her run in behind me. "We're here to see Mr. Tobias. He was brought in by ambulance. His nurse was probably with him. Ummm... Nurse Paige."

My mom looked over at me, surprised I knew so much. "Yes, she's right over there."

I ran to her. "Nurse Paige, remember me?"

"Yes. You've come to see him? I wish he could've told you how much you brightened his days. I don't know what happened. It's bad this time." Her eyes watered. "It's not like one of those times when he was faking it just to get back here. I think he had a crush on the nurses or something. This time something came over him. He couldn't breathe."

Something?

A nurse called her over and whispered to her. She covered her mouth and looked around the room as the nurse spoke. She nodded, looked back at me, held up a finger, and followed her back.

"What do you think happened?"

"I don't know," my mom replied. "That didn't look good."

"Can I go back there? Will they allow it?"

My mom did something unexpected. She walked up to the counter, and I couldn't be prouder that she was my mom. "Can we go back and see Mr. Tobias? This is his granddaughter."

"Let me check."

My mom sat down next to me. She watched the woman.

The receptionist spoke softly to someone. "She says she's his granddaughter. I don't know..."

A few minutes later, they waved us back.

We walked past several curtains that I didn't purposely look through, but they were parted. A man sat with a huge gash in his leg, a woman looked as if she'd passed out, and another woman had some kind of breathing tube in her mouth.

Further down the hall, Nurse Paige stood outside a curtain pulled closed, blocking off my view. She cried, "He's gone, sweetie. I'm sorry."

"No, he can't be." I ran toward the curtain.

My mom tried to pull me back. "Sheena!"

I ducked under the curtain and froze in place, looking at his lifeless body. His coloring was gone. He looked like a shell, like the part of him that made him *him* was missing.

"Do you have something to tell me? You were supposed to help me through this." I walked toward him and placed my hands on the bed rail. "You were the only person that understood—that could help me. You can't be gone. Get up. We have to go. We'll take you home."

"No, Sheena. What are you saying?"

I fought to get out of my mom's grasp. "Where are you?" I yelled up at the ceiling. "I know you're here. Help him! Bring him back!"

"Sheena, stop it. Come on, we're leaving."

"But I didn't find out what he wanted to tell me. He said there would be time to discuss everything, but there wasn't." I turned to Nurse Paige. "I don't even know what that last thing was he yelled out to me when you were running to catch the bus."

"Ask your friend."

"What?" I asked. "My friend doesn't know what he said. We couldn't hear him."

"No, that's what he yelled out to you. I only heard part of the question. You asked something like can they take, and he replied, 'Ask you friend.'" He laughed about it after we were on the bus. He said something like, 'I can't believe she doesn't know.'"

"Ask...my...friend? Which...friend?" It was hard to get the words out. My chest felt tight, and I was breathing too fast.

"Sheena…"

I was now at the foot of Mr. Tobias's bed, and looking just over his head. My eyes widened as I looked up to the ceiling. My mouth dropped open.

My mom looked back and forth from me to the ceiling. "What's wrong?" she asked.

Nurse Paige stepped closer to me. "She may be having an absence seizure."

I continued looking up at the being that fully formed and dipped his head toward me. His arms opened out to the sides, and as he did so, slight translucent wings appeared behind him. He brought his hands together, palms up, and dipped them down at Mr. Tobias's head. Something glowed there, within his forehead, as if the sun had been planted there, and its rays were releasing or escaping from a dark prison for all to see.

The being scooped it up as if gently lifting a bubble from water. With his palms together, he held his arms out toward me.

"What? No." Did he want me to take it? I stumbled back a couple of steps.

Nurse Paige rushed toward me with her arms outstretched.

"Don't touch me," I whispered. I don't know how I knew, but at that moment, no one could touch me.

Nurse Paige stopped. My mom slowly stepped closer, as if not to alarm me.

I don't think I had a choice in what was about to happen. The angel moved forward without walking. Standing ten feet tall, he brought his arms down over me, and the glowing thing—swirling light in the form of a tiny dove that under different circumstances I would've been intrigued about—lowered onto my head.

I saw a flash of light, but I didn't feel anything.

"Sheena," my mom said.

I touched my lip, feeling something wet there, and looked down at the drops of blood on my fingers.

"Her nose," said Nurse Paige as she reached for tissues.

I stared at my fingers. *Why am I bleeding? Am I dying?* I looked up at my mom. Her eyes were filled with concern and fear. My bloodied fingers reached for her, and she reached for me. I didn't get to feel the comfort of her embrace.

Darkness closed in around me as I slipped away.

BUT THERE'S MORE...

Please Leave A Review

Your review means the world to me. I greatly appreciate any kind words. Even one or two sentences go a long way. The number of reviews a book receives greatly improves how well it does on Amazon. Thank you in advance.

The adventure continues.
Turn the page to start reading book two,
The Girl Who Spoke to the Wind.

THE GIRL

WHO SPOKE
TO

THE WIND

The Sheena Meyer Series

Book Two

*Y*ou *must reflect the light of the sun, Gleamer.*
That's what I heard as I opened my eyes and looked
around the hospital room.

*Speak to the wind...speak to the wind...speak to the
wind...*The voice echoed. Mr. Tobias's voice.

"I don't understand," I whispered as my eyes slowly
blinked open. *Where am I?* I tried to sit up.

"Wait, Sheena," my mom said, gently pushing me back.

I looked down at the hospital bed, around the room, and
at the closed curtain.

"Are you okay?" my mom asked. She looked worried and
exhausted, like she had when my dad was in the hospital—
the same tension in her face.

I tried to sit up again.

"Hold on, Sheena," she said. "You fainted."

"I did?" I'd never fainted before. "I'm sorry."

"Why are you sorry? You don't have to apologize. How do you feel? Do you remember why we came to the hospital?"

I thought for a moment, my eyes searching the white tiles of the ceiling. I closed my eyes. Sorrowful, I replied, "Mr. Tobias. He's gone."

The curtain pulled back with a hard screech and someone entered. A male voice spoke to my mom. He sounded especially chipper as he came around the bed where I could see him and touched my arm.

"Are we okay now? I hear you lost consciousness."

I looked up at the gentle expression and bright eyes of Nurse Javan. His sparkled just like Mr. Tobias's, like...Ariel's. If my assumption was right...

I sat up totally alert, shocked he was there. "Do you remember me?"

"Let's see...You were here late one night. I think you were going to your dad's room," he replied with a warm grin.

"Yes." I was so glad he didn't mention I was talking to myself.

"I'm usually pretty good with faces."

"How are you with answers?"

"I will give you whatever information I can. Knowledge is important. It is only what you know that can save you."

"Save me from what?"

"Anything." He read over a chart and looked up at me with a grin. "Everything."

"Does that mean what you don't know can kill you?"

""Maybe." He looked into my eyes as if he wanted me to really understand what he was saying. "But I know you don't have to worry about that because you're going to study hard and learn as much as you can. You're special, I can tell," he said with a wink. "You've been given everything you need to become very successful and conquer whatever comes against you."

Given? That's when I remembered everything that happened before I fainted. What was the glowing thing the angel took from Mr. Tobias and gave to me? Was it something to help me?

"Is that why I'm supposed to speak to the wind?" I asked with a brow raised. "What does that mean?"

Nurse Javan smiled. "The wind? Uh, okay."

Oh no! He had no idea what I'd been talking about. *I thought he was*— "Wait. Rewind. That didn't come out right. That was, uh, something crazy I heard someone say. Ha! Like someone would actually talk to the wind. That's crazy, right?"

I slumped back against the pillow and stared at my hands in my lap, avoiding my mom's frown. She had looked back and forth at us, confused. I'm sure she thought I might have hit my head when I collapsed and awoke talking crazy, or in riddles or something.

Nurse Javan turned to my mom. "I know Doctor Davies has already spoken to you. Since her electrocardiogram results are fine, no hospitalization is necessary."

"That means I can go?"

"You sure can."

A half-hour later, my mom and I stood outside the hospital emergency room entrance. Our car sat at the end of the sidewalk, but my mom didn't walk toward it.

"Sheena, I'm kind of dumbfounded right now. Maybe we've been too lax with you because of how responsible you usually are. It's like you have a whole other life going on that I know nothing about. How is that possible? You're just a child."

"I'm not a child." I knew as soon as I said it that I shouldn't have.

"Trust, now is not a good time for you to test me. And your dad..." She threw her hand up. "I don't even know how to begin to explain this to him." She looked down at her phone. "That's him now. I'm letting it go to voicemail. I'm not ready to have that conversation yet."

"What are you doing? I thought you weren't ready to tell him anything?"

"A little something is better than nothing at all. I'm texting him that everything is fine and that I'll explain later. Hopefully that will pacify him for now." She placed her phone in her purse. "Now tell me what in the world all of that was about? Start with Mr. Tobias. I know you care—"

"I don't care! I don't care anymore! I mean, I care about Mr. Tobias, but I didn't ask for any of this. And I'm so confused."

"Didn't ask for any of what?"

I looked into my mom's brown eyes. *Should I tell her? Would it put her in danger? Would she think I was crazy and send me off to an asylum or something like they did with Mr. Tobias when he was young?*

"Sheena, what is it? You can talk to me. You can tell me anything." Her eyes pleaded with me.

"Mom, sit down."

We sat on the silver benches that were meant for those waiting for their rides to pull up after being discharged from the hospital.

"What's going on?"

There was no easy way to tell her, so I just blurted it out. "Mom, I-I see things."

She had been facing me. Holding my hands and looking into my eyes. She turned away, looking out at the parking lot across from the hospital.

She didn't ask any questions, laugh, or freak out. Maybe she hadn't heard me or misunderstood, so I repeated it. "I see things."

She grabbed my hand again. "I heard you the first time. Let's go for a ride."

I didn't say anything further. I just wanted to know what she was thinking—whether she believed me or not. And why didn't she ask for details? I know my statement had major shock factor, but she showed no signs of its impact.

Neither of us spoke on the drive. I watched her, thinking I could read her expression and know what she was thinking, but I couldn't.

Maybe the angel granted me some type of mindreading power, I thought as I stared at her, pushing with my brain. Nothing happened. No superpowers. I was still just a teenager that had no idea where she fit in the scheme of the world.

Mentally exhausted, I fell asleep after a while. When I awoke, we were pulling in front of a yellow house surrounded by open fields.

Nothing ever changes here, I thought as I got out of the car and looked around.

The screened front door of the house opened. "My babies!"

My mom walked into her open arms. Then I stepped forward for her embrace, pressing the side of my face into the shoulder of her light blue house dress and inhaling the familiar gardenia scent of her favorite lotion.

"Hi Nana."

"It's so good to see my baby. My, you look more and more like my mother, your great grandmother, every time I see you. Get on in this house. Don't you feel that chill?"

We walked in, laughing after Nana saying something about it starting to get chilly enough to see chill bumps on a gnat.

But Nana didn't follow us in. She stood at the door for a minute, looking out over the field across the street before closing the door.

"Mama, is everything okay?" my mom asked Nana.

"A storm is coming," she mumbled.

I looked out the window. There wasn't a cloud in the sky.

As Nana and my mom talked in the living room, I did what I'd done for as long as I could remember, walked straight to the back of the house to the kitchen to see if—

Yes! I exclaimed in my head. There was a three-layer cake with tan frosting sitting in the center of the kitchen table, covered with a glass top.

"Sheena? Don't you touch that caramel cake!" Nana yelled.

"Omkay," is how my response sounded. My mouth was already full.

Nana and my mom walked into the kitchen laughing a few minutes later, talking about me, knowing what I would do when I saw the cake.

"Why don't we all have a slice, and I'll make tea. It seems that we have some things to discuss."

"Mom, you told her?" I whispered.

Nana put the kettle on the stove. "You focus on the wrong things, sweetie. The question is why she told me, and why she brought you here after you told her."

I looked down at my cake. I hadn't thought about that. I wondered if Nana had superhuman hearing, or if I was that bad of a whisperer.

My mom sat at my left under a wall of old copper pans Nana collected. She stood to help Nana with the tea infuser and cups.

I imagined myself as a kid running through the kitchen while Nana cooked and being scolded for it. A huge pot of mixed greens boiled on the stove and Nana stood over the counter seasoning meat. I remember being horrified because I thought she was cooking a puppy. I was ready to run away because of it and live on Sesame Street. Not the actual street, but the television show.

Coon is what she called it. *Coon?* My eyes widened in alarm. I just realized she meant racoon. My stomach turned a flip. *Did I eat any of it? I couldn't have. I didn't like the texture of meat back then.*

Why were all of these memories just coming back to me?

Everything in the room was the same as back then, except for the addition of some new kitchen gadgets on the counter. I remember my mom having to intervene last year regarding Nana's shopping channel obsession.

I finished up my cake just as Nana and my mom were beginning to eat theirs.

"Now, tell Nana what you saw."

She looked at me over her glasses, and I realized I'd never been able to keep anything from her. Nana asked with that penetrating gaze of hers, and I told her whatever she wanted to know.

"I don't know where to start. I feel overwhelmed."

"I'm sure. Maybe this will help."

Nana placed another slice of cake on my plate. She laughed. "It's always helped in the past to calm you down when you were upset.

"Chew slowly this time," Nana instructed.

There was some connection between chewing slowly, and the creamy frosting, I think, that soothes. I took a huge bite and talked with my mouth full. "Eyef baw some ak hospit." I added another fork full of cake to my already stuffed mouth. "Aww hink was angem."

Milk. I need milk. I grabbed my glass and drank in huge gulps. *BURP!* "Excuse me."

Nana nodded. "Slow down. Take a deep breath, sweetie."

I did as I was told.

"I think I caught a little of what you were saying. Ha! Glory be, I have no idea how."

I loved Nana's laugh. It was high-pitched and bouncy. The kind of laugh that if you heard it you could do nothing but laugh also. Just hearing it comforted me.

"I have no idea what that was," my mom said. "Let's try that again."

"She said she thinks she saw an angel at the hospital." Nana turned to me. "Is that right, sweetie?"

"I nodded."

"Tell us about Mr. Tobias," my mom instructed. I took a deep breath and told them everything. Everything except about sneaking out of the house. I mean, I'm not crazy or anything.

Nana didn't seem surprised by anything I said. It was like she heard this kind of stuff every day. It made it easier to talk to her, but still, I wondered why she didn't react in some way.

Instead, Nana said, "Belinda, you were supposed to pay close attention to her."

"I have been, Mama," my mom replied.

I looked back and forth between them. *Wait, what? What's going on?* It was like they knew something was going to happen to me. Like they expected it...

ABOUT THE AUTHOR

L. B. Anne is best known for her Lolo and Winkle book series in which she tells humorous stories of middle-school siblings, Lolo and Winkle, based on her youth, growing up in Queens, New York. She lives on the Gulf Coast of Florida with her husband and is a full-time author and speaker. When she's not inventing new obstacles for her diverse characters to overcome, you can find her reading, playing bass guitar, running on the beach, or downing a mocha iced coffee at a local cafe while dreaming of being your favorite author.

Visit L. B. at www.lbanne.com

Facebook: facebook.com/authorlbanne

Instagram: Instagram.com/authorlbanne

Twitter: twitter.com/authorlbanne

Printed in Germany
by Amazon Distribution
GmbH, Leipzig

17195549R00106